Celia's
Robot

Celia's Robot

MARGARET CHANG

Holiday House / New York

Library of Congress Cataloging-in-Publication Data

Chang, Margaret Scrogin.
Celia's robot / by Margaret Chang. — 1st ed.
p. cm.
Summary: Surprised by her scientist father's gift of a robot for her birthday,
ten-year-old Celia comes to appreciate its help in organizing her chaotic
day-to-day life until it suddenly mysteriously disappears.
ISBN 978-0-8234-2181-7 (hardcover)
[1. Robots—Fiction.   2. Friendship—Fiction.   3. Family life—Fiction.   4. Racially
mixed people—Fiction.   5. Chinese Americans—Fiction.]   I. Title.
PZ7.C359667Ce 2009
[Fic]—dc22
2009007555

To Raymond,
the one-man ground crew
for my first solo flight.
I couldn't have done it
without you.

Contents

Celia's
Robot

1

My Messed-Up Morning

"Celia, you're late!" Dad was shaking my bed by its foot-board. "You should be up and dressed by now. Your breakfast is getting cold!"

The first time Dad checked on me after the alarm rang, he tried to wake me up by playing the music box he made for my ninth birthday last year. It was really neat. The ballerina on top danced in rhythm to the Sugar Plum Fairy's music from *The Nutcracker*. Mom sewed her tiny net dress, but Dad had made her legs move. I listened to the bright, chiming notes and stayed in bed, half asleep, remembering other presents from other birthdays.

Every year I got something new—Dad works with computers and loves inventing things. When I turned five, he gave me a sneaker that sang instructions about how to tie my shoes, with the lace holes flashing green if I was doing it right, and red if I wasn't. A year later, Dad designed a special computer game, with me as the avatar. He made the characters in my favorite stories teach me things like math and spelling, but mostly I liked being inside each story. I could rescue Peter Rabbit, trick the wicked wolf, or fly with Wendy. Another year Dad built a train with a cat face to carry my china animals on journeys around my room. The caboose had a poofy tail that doubled as a duster when the train went under my desk or by my bookshelves.

I was drifting back to sleep, wondering whatever happened to that train, when Dad stomped back in to yell and shake my bed. He could make me laugh like no one else could, but that morning he was in no mood for jokes.

Dad stayed to watch me get up this time, then went back into his bedroom to finish dressing. A good thing Mom would be back tonight. She never got impatient as quickly as Dad did. She'd been on tour in Texas with her string quartet, Calyx, for the past week, leaving Dad and me on our own.

It was the coldest morning since school had started. I looked around for my robe, then remembered that I'd stuffed it in the closet when Dad made me clean up my room last weekend. I'd shoved so much junk in there that I hadn't dared to open it since. I found my down jacket under my desk, wrapped it around me, pulled on a couple of dirty mismatched socks to keep my feet warm, and shuffled out of my room to the breakfast bar.

My oatmeal was waiting for me, all congealed in the bowl. I poured milk over it anyway, took a bite, and almost gagged on the cold lump in my mouth. When I reached for orange juice to wash it down, I knocked over the glass. I'm always slow and clumsy in the mornings.

The juice splashed over my toast, running down the counter to soak my pajamas and jacket.

"Celia," Dad yelled from the bedroom, "get going. You don't have much time!"

Now that Mrs. Boyer, our old housekeeper, was in Arizona with her married daughter, I was supposed to make my own lunch while Mom was touring. Sometimes I actually did, but there wasn't enough time today. My wet pajamas stuck to my skin as I hurried back to my room, throwing my jacket on top of the bathroom's hamper on my way.

What would I wear to school? I wasn't about to open my closet. I looked at the clothes tumbled over the floor and pulled on a pair of pants. They would look okay under the dress I wore yesterday, which was draped over my desk chair.

The book I'd been reading last night, about a tough girl who stole money and ran away from her fat foster mother, lay facedown on the floor. Would she actually get on that bus to California, where she'd meet her real mother? I picked it up. I only meant to read a page or two, but then Pablo crawled up on my lap and went to sleep. He's a Siamese cat, and loves people. Mom says he thinks I'm his mother. I couldn't disturb him, could I?

"Celia, are you dressed? I'm ready to leave!" Dad shouted from the front door. He works in Cambridge, and sometimes it takes him an hour to drive there. He likes to leave early to beat the traffic and get a parking place.

I jumped up and pulled off my dirty socks. Pablo

landed on his feet and licked his back, looking insulted. I tossed one sock up into my globe light. It didn't land inside, so I tried the other one. Success!

Dad rushed down the hall to see what was holding me up. He stood in my doorway and shouted, "It's seven-thirty, and you're not dressed!"

When Dad is angry, his face gets red and he gets all tight-looking, especially around his mouth.

I pulled the dress over my head. "Yes I am," I said.

His eyes went wide and he yelled, "Oh, no you're not! You don't have your shoes on. That dress is wrinkled and there's paint on the front. You must have something clean." He opened the door to my closet.

"Don't—" I started to say, but I couldn't stop him in time.

Two dirty nightgowns, a large Raggedy Ann doll, a bag of yarn, and a small loom tumbled down around Dad's feet. The pieces of an old lock I'd been taking apart almost hit his head. He quickly pushed my closet door shut, before Lego blocks, puzzle boxes, and a bunch of hangers could follow the lock.

"That dress will have to do till Mom gets back," he said. "Where are your shoes? Your room looks like a hazardous waste dump!"

I felt really stupid. I couldn't remember where I'd left my shoes, so I guessed. "I think they're in the living room."

"I'll find them. You need to comb your hair." Dad ran down the hall.

I went to the bathroom and grabbed my comb. Mom

had French braided my hair before she left, but the braids were coming loose. In the bathroom light, my black hair really did have red highlights, just like my Chinese grandmother, Zumu, says. She's always telling me how American I look. But since I'm the only Asian-looking kid at Abigail Adams Elementary, everyone there thinks I'm Chinese. Mom has blond hair, so when we're together, people usually think I'm adopted. Once a guy in a museum asked, "Where did you get her?" Mom just smiled and answered, "In the usual way."

While I was trying to decide whether to pull my braids apart and wear a headband, the telephone rang from somewhere in my bedroom. I'd been talking to Mom in Texas last night and never put the phone back. I found it under my bed, just as the answering machine was kicking in.

"Hello, hello!" I shouted over Dad's recorded voice: *"You have two minutes to leave a message."*

"Hey, Celia." It was Jen. "What are you wearing to the museum today?"

My heart sank. I'd completely forgotten we had a field trip.

"Gotta find my permission slip," I told her. "See you."

I had just pressed the End button when Dad stormed back from the living room. "Looked all over. Shoes not there." He spoke fast and loud, as if he were talking to Zumu in Chinese.

I tried to remember taking off my shoes. Maybe I'd shoved them under my bed? Yes, there they were!

Dad dumped my backpack in front of me. "Quick, put in your books. Where's your coat?"

"In the bathroom." I shivered with cold and a little bit of panic because I was so late.

"Meet you at the door with your coat." Dad rushed down the hall.

I jammed my books and homework papers into my backpack. I couldn't make my books fit. My backpack was such an awkward jumble that I felt like crying.

Standing by the door, Dad asked, "What's on your coat?"

"Orange juice."

"How did—never mind! Need your violin today?"

I was so mixed up by all the yelling and rushing I couldn't remember what day it was, so I asked.

The way Dad sighed made me feel even dumber. "It's Wednesday."

"Wednesday is Suzuki class, so I need it." On Mondays and Wednesdays I get released from regular music class for beginning Suzuki method violin lessons.

"Well, then, get your violin. And hurry!" Dad held the doorknob, ready to open the front door so I could run out.

I dashed to my bedroom. Pablo put his ears back and dived under my bed. I had no idea where I'd put my violin, so I dug down under the dress-up clothes and pile of drawings behind my easel. No violin.

"I must have left it at school!" I shouted at Dad as I ran out the door.

"Hurry or you'll miss the bus!" he called after me. He would reset the security system and put Pablo in the basement before he drove out of the garage.

As I ran down Heartwright Lane, almost out of breath, I heard vicious barking. Rocky the killer dog helps guard the Heartwright Estate across the street from us. I looked sideways to make sure that Rocky was on the other side of the estate's tall iron fence. I knew he could kill me as easily as he once killed the Levins' barn cats.

Distracted by Rocky, I missed a big crack in the road, tripped, and went sprawling. My books fell out of my backpack. As I gathered them up, I felt stinging on one knee and palm. I didn't even look down to see if my pants were torn. I got up and ran for the bus.

By the time I reached the corner of Woodland Road, the school bus was already roaring away. Mrs. Flynt, the driver, couldn't see me, but Tim O'Mara looked out the back window. He pulled his eyes so they slanted and I could see him mouthing, "Chinky, Chinky." What a jerk!

I turned around. I would have to go back and face Dad. My backpack seemed to weigh a ton. Now my knee really hurt, and my palm was on fire.

Then I heard a loud, impatient honk. Dad's Volvo pulled up beside me. I opened the back door to slide in. There, on the back seat, was my violin.

"Left it in the car on Monday." Dad sighed, shaking his head. He had picked me up after school that day, when I'd missed the bus because I'd spent too long gabbing with

Jen. From where I sat, Dad looked tired and a little sad. Not at all like the guy who made everyone laugh at his company picnic last weekend. I had heard Mr. Weissman, who owns Moria Systems, say to a young guy they'd just hired, "That Alex Chow, he's a screwball, but he'll work out the vision problem, you'll see." Dad designs robots for Moria and he's a big shot there, but then he'd been clowning around, which always surprises people who don't know him. Dad told me later that most people expect Chinese to be serious and inscrutable.

Because Dad drives me to school by the quickest route, we arrived before the custodians unlocked the doors. He was still impatient to get to work, even though he'd lost the early start he wanted.

"Good-bye, Celia. Don't forget your violin," Dad said over his shoulder as I got out the back door. He sounded weary.

Dad gunned his motor and drove off. As I caught my breath, I remembered that I still didn't have my permission slip, and that I'd forgotten to ask Dad for lunch money. Plus, we were supposed to bring in a written proposal for our science project today, and I didn't have one. And I was pretty sure I'd left my math homework on my bedroom floor. All in all, this had to be the worst morning since I'd started fifth grade.

Sitting there, waiting for Jennifer and Maeve in my sticky coat and with blood running down my knee, I felt like a great big zero. I was afraid Dad might be so mad he wouldn't make anything for my birthday, just a few weeks off. After the morning I'd had, he probably thought I would just lose it or break it. I would never have imagined, not in a million years, the big idea that hit Dad while he was stuck in traffic on that crazy, messed-up morning.

2

My Birthday

"Leave me alone," I yelled at Tim's back. He had "accidentally" bumped me as we got off the bus. He looked back and waved, grinning obnoxiously, as he trotted up the private driveway that ran from his back door up to the mansion's carriage house. Meanwhile Rocky rushed down the grassy hill to growl angrily at me through the iron fence. Tim worked at the Heartwright Estate after school, helping Mark Ludlow rake leaves. Mark took care of the estate for Mrs. Prentice, who spends most of her time in Florida. He and Rocky lived over the carriage house.

The afternoon turned so warm that I'd taken off my torn pants at recess and stuffed them inside my backpack. I started down Heartwright Lane, holding my stained jacket, enjoying the soft air on my bare legs. Music from a string quartet floated up from the end of the lane, along with the smell of baking bread. My heart seemed to rise with the music as I started to run. I forgot all about Tim and Rocky. Mom was home!

The front door was open a crack. I ran in, dumping

my coat and backpack on the floor. Mom came out of the guest room and swept me up in a big hug. Wet hair hung over her shoulder, and she smelled like she'd just taken a shower.

I'd really missed her. Without Mrs. Boyer, the house had seemed empty and lonely. Dad had worked late every afternoon, trying to solve the vision problem, and had stayed in his workshop with the door closed the rest of the time, while I was supposed to be cleaning up my room. I didn't have anyone to talk to but Pablo, since I'm an only child.

"One is enough," Mom sometimes said, but she always hugged me when she said it.

That afternoon, as she stepped back from our hug, Mom looked at my dress, then down at the wet hair falling in front of her shoulder. Her blond hair had soaked up blue paint from the front of my dress.

"Isn't that the same dress you wore the day I left?" Mom asked.

My throat closed up. I could only nod.

"Celia, I left clean T-shirts and jeans hanging in your closet." When her voice went high and irritated like that, my insides got all twisted up.

I gulped. "Dad made me tidy up my room and I couldn't get into the closet afterward."

"Celia, how many times, *how many times*, have I asked you to clean out your closet? Why won't you ever do it?"

Mom went into the kitchen and leaned over the sink, closing her eyes and sighing as she held her blue hair under a running faucet. She grabbed a kitchen towel to dry it. When she turned around, she managed a small smile. Her irritation vanished with the blue paint. I followed her and took a seat at the breakfast bar, where a loaf of banana bread sat cooling.

"I'll look into your closet tomorrow," Mom said. While she poured herself a cup of coffee and me a glass of milk, she sighed again and repeated something she'd said a million times before. "I wish Mrs. Boyer hadn't left town."

I grabbed a knife and cut myself a thick slice of banana bread. My stomach was positively growling.

"What happened to your hand?" Mom asked.

"I tripped and fell while I was running to the bus. Skinned my knee, too. Mrs. Flower let me go to the nurse's office."

I didn't tell Mom that I rested there for almost two hours while the other fifth graders went on an art field trip to the D'Avila Museum.

"Oh, Celia, that must have hurt! We'll put on a new bandage tonight before you go to bed." Then, seeing me cut another slice of banana bread, she asked, "What did you make for your lunch today?"

"I got lunch at school. It wasn't very good." That was partly true, because Maeve and Jen and Alison gave me parts of their lunches. Thinking I'd better distract her from any more questions, I asked, "How was the tour?"

"Small audiences. To make things worse, on the very

first night the Houston paper sent some kid who didn't know a thing about classical music, and he wrote a terrible review that got published all over."

Mom hates bad reviews.

"I missed you and Dad, and I don't want to think about playing in Canada." Her next tour started the day after my birthday.

Mom stared at me for a moment, then added, "Looks like you and Dad didn't do too well while I was gone."

I shrugged and cut a smaller slice of banana bread. "We did okay."

Since Mom didn't ask, I didn't tell her that Mrs. Flower gave me a zero in math because I forgot my homework again, and that she'd told me if I didn't have an idea for a science project in by tomorrow, she would be calling Mom and Dad for a conference.

Trying for something that would keep Mom from asking more about my day at school, I said, "Tim O'Mara is such a pest! When he got on the bus coming home, he yelled, 'Hey stupid, who's your ugly friend?' at me and Maeve."

Mom looked like she was trying not to laugh. "Tim called *you* stupid and *Maeve* ugly?" she asked. "Two of the smartest and prettiest girls in the fifth grade?" She put her arm around me. "He can say anything he likes. You don't have to believe him. I bet he's just trying to get your attention."

I didn't tell her that after Tim took a seat at the back

of the bus, Maeve and I spent the rest of the ride thinking up ways to kill him. We made up a plan to lure Tim and Rocky into our garage and lock them in together.

Mom sipped the last of her coffee. "Dad called after I got home to say he'd be late tonight, because he's assembling equipment he needs to work on an idea he had today. After all that banana bread, you won't mind a late dinner, and we can call Grandmary and Grandpop while we're waiting." Mom picked up the kitchen phone to dial the long number.

When it's evening in West Haven, it's morning in Shandong, China, where Grandpop was spending his sabbatical. (He's a college professor, and they get a year off every so often.) I leaned against Mom, listening as she told her parents about Calyx's tour of Texas.

"Don't pay attention to ignorant reviewers," Grandpop told Mom.

When Mom handed me the phone, Grandmary told me, "Your tape just arrived. It's grand to hear your voice."

Grandpop added, "We like your e-mails, too. You write very well."

I nibbled on banana bread crumbs while Mom kept talking. I really missed Grandmary and Grandpop, but I think Mom missed them even more. They'd always lived two hours away, in the town where Mom grew up. Grandmary usually came to visit when Mom was on tour. She'd sleep in the guest room so that she could pick me up at school, take me to the library, make me dinner, and put me to bed when Dad worked late. I could invite Maeve and Jen over when she visited, or she'd drive me to their houses. Grandmary came to stay when Mom was around, too. In winter, she'd bring a huge puzzle for us to work on. In warmer seasons, the three of us would go for bird walks near Walden Pond. In every season, we often sat down for afternoon tea, and Mom and Grandmary would talk about books and people and music.

With Mrs. Boyer and Grandmary gone, the house looked messier, but Mom seemed messier, too. She spent more time practicing, or staring off into space, or e-mailing and phoning Grandmary and Grandpop. She still made breakfast, but we ate a lot of take-out dinners. She and I didn't play so many duets, and when we did, it was like she didn't hear me.

After Mom finished talking, she told me to set the table while she started dinner. I had just finished feeding Pablo when I heard Dad's key in the door, and then a scrape and a loud thump.

"Celia," Dad yelled, "why did you leave your backpack where anyone can trip over it? Come hang up your coat!"

Two gray plastic trunks sat in the vestibule. They had some kind of combination lock, but I never got a good look, because Dad took the trunks straight to his workroom. He'd brought home stuff to work on before, but never so much at once as this.

"What's all that for?" I asked Mom.

She pursed her lips and kept her eyes on the lettuce

leaves she was tearing apart for salad. "He's got an idea for a new prototype he wants to keep secret," was all she said.

As soon as we were all settled at dinner, Mom said, "Alex, I really should call Mrs. Le Beck tomorrow so we can get started interviewing for a new housekeeper."

Mom had already talked about hiring a new house-keeper, but Dad kept putting her off.

Sure enough, Dad looked down at his plate. "What's the rush? You'll be here until Celia's birthday."

"Alex, we really need to line up someone we trust to stay with Celia after school and tidy up. Especially now that my parents are in China, and I've got so many tours ahead." Mom put down her fork and knife and stared at Dad, trying to get him to look at her. "Celia had a really hard time while I was in Texas. Her clothes are all dirty. She missed lunch today. Her room's even worse. And her hair's a mess."

Dad concentrated on his food, not answering. He didn't come right out and say so, but Mom and I knew he didn't want some strange new person in the house. Mrs. Boyer had worked for us before he built the workshop, so he trusted her.

Mom took a deep breath and addressed the issue head-on. "You don't have to be so paranoid," she said. "After all, your workshop has its own security system. And you said you built it so you could spend more time here."

"I think Celia can get along without a sitter for now," Dad answered, as if he never thought of his workshop.

"Now that I've made so much progress on the vision problem, I'll be working on a new application at home."

Mom looked skeptical. "After vision, you'll have another crisis," she predicted. But she didn't say anything more about calling Mrs. Le Beck's housekeeping service.

Mom always told me that Dad was used to getting his own way because he was the only boy growing up in a Chinese family.

After dinner, Mom went to the guest room to play one of her favorite pieces, and Dad locked himself in his workroom. I put my ear to his door. I could hear an orchestra playing on the ancient radio Dad built before I was born. Live Bach from Mom in one ear, recorded Brahms from Dad in the other. Confusing. I couldn't see anything, but I could smell hot plastic and solvent and hear the whine of his drill, the ring of metal against metal, and the thud of plastic against plastic. After a few minutes I got bored and wandered back to my bedroom to fiddle with Dad's old MindMate. Mom stopped playing and came in to check on my homework, which I hadn't started.

As the trees along Heartwright Lane turned color and lost their leaves, I began to wonder. Was Dad working on some project for Moria Systems or on a birthday surprise for me?

Several times, I tried to ask him what he was doing. He would only say he was building a prototype and I shouldn't tell anyone about it. I was afraid I'd sound stupid if I asked what *prototype* meant. Much later I found out it means "first try." Dad told me he was working at home because Mr. Weissman was afraid some guy named Christian Fisher would try to steal his secret discoveries in robotics.

I listened at the door every night while Mom was practicing. One night, I thought I heard my own voice through the door, telling Grandmary and Grandpop about the beginning of fifth grade. Why would Dad have a copy of the tape I sent them? He knew what was going on at school.

If only Pablo could talk. He loved to sneak into Dad's workroom, and Dad always let him stay.

My birthday fell on a Sunday. Zumu arrived from Brookline in the late afternoon. She wore a pale green pantsuit to match her jade ring, and carried a shopping bag. "More boxes in the car," she told Dad.

The wrapped presents Grandmary and Grandpop had left behind before they went to China were already stacked on the coffee table. I recognized the hard, solid shape of books and the rattling sound of new puzzles.

Mom rolled her eyes behind Zumu's back. At breakfast she had said, "I hope your mother doesn't go overboard. Celia has too much stuff already."

"At least she hasn't bugged us to have a boy," Dad had answered. Zumu told me her Chinese friends sometimes say it's too bad her only grandchild is a girl. "You best," she always says. "Things different in America."

When Zumu smiles, she glows, and at that moment

she turned all her light on me. "Ten is an important birthday," she said. She held out a small box from the shopping bag just as Dad walked in, carrying a stack of larger boxes.

"Let's put everything in the living room," Mom said, looking at the stack with dismay.

I opened Zumu's little box first. Inside was a silk pouch that closed with a loop and fancy knot, and inside that was a pair of small jade earrings. "I wore them when I was your age," Zumu said.

I cradled them, gold and jade, on my palm, thinking Zumu had carried them all the way from Shanghai to Taiwan to Brookline. "Mom, can I have my ears pierced soon?" I asked.

Mom sighed. "Maybe it's time," she said. But she didn't sound like she meant it.

"I know someone in Brookline who'll do a good job," Zumu offered. I put the earrings back in their pouch and started opening my other presents. Mom went into the kitchen to make tea. Zumu always gives me lots of nice clothes. This time she gave me a new dress, a jumper with a matching blouse, a new sweater, and three fancy tops for my jeans. She teaches Chinese classes, so she gave me a tape and book to help me learn Chinese, and a new board game to play with my friends. I opened Grandmary's books and the puzzles she picked out, but I was too distracted to look at them carefully. I kept wondering about my present from Dad and Mom.

Supper seemed to last forever. My parents and Zumu

chatted and sipped wine as if they had nothing else to do. Mom brought out a chocolate fudge cake—my favorite—and I blew out ten candles. I kept worrying that Dad thought I didn't deserve a special surprise for my birthday.

Dad doesn't like sweets, but he ate a little cake because it was my birthday. When we were all finished, he said, "Let's go back to the living room."

What was going on? I knew he hadn't put anything in the living room while we were eating. The presents I had unwrapped were still spread out on the glass coffee table. Paper and ribbon still littered the floor. Newspapers and magazines were still piled under the piano, where Dad had pushed them earlier. Pablo still slept peacefully next to the hot air vent.

Dad looked very pleased with himself. "Close your eyes," he told me. "Don't open them until I say so."

I heard Dad walk down to his workroom. I heard him press the code buttons and the workshop door slide open. Still I kept my eyes closed. I heard whirring, then a muffled sound. It sounded like a loaded wagon rolling over the slate floor in the vestibule, the hardwood floor in the living room, and then the oriental carpet in the living room, and toward me. Still I kept my eyes closed.

"Now open your eyes!" Dad said.

3

Robot Arrives

A canister of black plastic about as high as my chest, topped by a silvery translucent plastic dome, stood in front of me. Two globes stuck out from the dome on short stems, its camcorder eyes. I thought they were so beautiful I wanted to touch them. They looked like glass, with a shimmery shining surface and depths of dark brown. Those "eyes" pointed straight at me, looking as surprised as I felt.

Between the eyes, a small window pulsed pale blue, to show the waves of sound that helped it figure out where it was. A long thin speaker embedded just under the dome would be its voice, and below that, a microphone, a robot ear, and a mysterious dark window. A tiny computer screen marked the spot where a person's heart would be. Tubes that looked like dryer hoses hung from its sides. Each "arm" ended in a "hand," with five curved pinchers on the left and articulated plastic fingers on the right. The whole thing rested on a small platform, which covered its wheels.

Dad had made a robot for my birthday present.

Zumu gasped and whispered in Chinese, something I didn't understand. She looked as startled as I was. Mom sat still, head down, idly leafing through one of the books from Grandmary. She must have known about the robot all along.

"This is my present?" I asked Dad. I was so amazed, I sounded like a squeaky baby.

"Speak to it. Introduce yourself," Dad said. "Only you can give it voice commands."

I noticed he held a remote control pad. I gulped, and while I was thinking what to say, it dawned on me that he must have used the remote to get the robot from his workroom to the living room.

"Hi, Robot," I said, feeling rather silly, talking to a plastic canister. "I'm Celia Chow."

Zumu looked puzzled and disapproving. Dad grinned, while Mom looked up from the book and put on her performer's smile, the one she uses to cover her real feelings.

The dome glowed a gentle blue. A synthesized voice came out of the speaker-mouth, enunciating each word in the same even tone. "I am pleased to meet you, Celia. I am your new robot."

Pablo skittered under the slouchy leather sofa to watch from underneath. When he's scared or excited, his pupils get so big, his eyes look black.

I didn't know what to answer. I just stood there, staring at the robot. I never thought I would have one of my own, one that wasn't a toy.

Dad was talking. "I've installed basic voice recognition software, keyed to your voice. Now you must talk to it. Teach it. I'll show you how."

I stood there with my mouth open, too amazed to be excited. I couldn't quite take in what Dad was saying. I even felt a little scared.

Dad turned to Zumu and Mom. "This robot will keep her safe when we're not here." Zumu said something in Chinese. It's hard to guess what people are saying in Chinese by their tone of voice, because Chinese comes out in bursts, and they always sound a little mad. Still, I thought Zumu didn't believe him.

"Good for your work," she said in English. "I take care of Celia better."

"Except that you teach every day," Dad shot back.

Mom didn't say anything. She stood up and walked to the side window, where she stared out at the tangle of leafless underbrush.

Dad grabbed my arm to get my attention. He wanted to show me what the robot could and couldn't do.

"This robot runs on batteries," he told me. "I've designed them to last all day, but they will need to be recharged at night. I'll put a recharger beside your bed. It can find its way there if it needs to." When Dad gets excited, he paces around. His clothes rumple up. Even his hair seems to stand up on its own.

He pointed to the small dark square. "You will see a red glow when information is being beamed by infrared light. The robot can communicate with your printer and other devices."

"There are many important safety features," Dad went on. I know this sounds like a commercial, but that's how Dad talked. Then he looked at Zumu again.

"I made it part of the house security system. It will turn the system on when we leave the house, and it will open the door for Celia when she comes home from school." Dad was very proud of his security system. He called it "fail safe" because he rigged the electrical locks to unlock if the power goes out, so we wouldn't be trapped inside.

To me, he said: "Tell it to follow you to your room. It is programmed to do what you do. Speak like you do to Pablo."

"Come with me," I said, clearly and distinctly. The window between its eyes pulsed with blue light. I started down the hall, looking over my shoulder. The robot wheeled around and followed me out of the living room and down the hall. It looked cross-eyed as it focused its eyes. I led it past the guest room and bathroom and into my room. We stood there looking at each other. Its dome swiveled, its eyes seemed to roll.

"Good job," I said to it.

The light between its eyes pulsed more brightly. "Dense with objects," the robot remarked.

It took me a minute to realize it meant my room. Then I heard Dad calling from the living room. "Lead it back."

"Let's go back," I said. I was beginning to feel all-powerful, like a teacher.

The robot turned around again and followed me into

the hallway, its blue lights gently throbbing. It circled the potted avocado tree, staying close behind me. Would it follow me if I took another way? I led it into the kitchen, past the long counter where we ate breakfast, now littered with dinner dishes, around the dining room table, and back into the living room. It followed right behind, avoiding the pile of newspapers. When we came to the oriental carpet, it lifted its base a little higher above its wheels, like it was walking tiptoe. Mom turned away from the window to watch it. She smiled, but her eyes looked sad.

"Stop!" I commanded, and it did, just before it reached the glass coffee table. Zumu, sitting at the end of the long sofa, looked relieved.

Dad started talking quickly, pacing around. "I've equipped it with sonar and radar, so it can find its way around most objects. I'm not sure yet how well it can make other discriminations." I was too excited to figure out what he meant. I did later, though.

Dad was talking fast because he had a lot more to tell me. "It can't go up or down stairs. If we take it outside, it will rise up higher to roll over dirt and grass. In case you need protection on Heartwright Lane, I've given it a special feature. You know how you're always worrying that Rocky could get out and bite you?"

He pulled me around behind the robot and pointed to a yellow button with the No sign, a circle crossed by a line, superimposed on the image of a dog. "When you press this, Robot will emit a high-pitched noise guaranteed to drive any dog away."

"I should show Pablo how to press it," I said, thinking of the kittens Rocky had killed. We never let Pablo out because of that awful dog.

Dad went on as if he hadn't heard me. I must not try to lift the robot, he told me.

"Good thing this house all on one floor," said Zumu.

"That's why we bought it." Mom returned to the sofa to sit beside Zumu. "Remember? It was built for a lawyer who used a wheelchair. Alex wanted a place to build robots at home."

Dad looked annoyed. He hated when Mom got off the subject. He really wanted to show off the robot. "It has eighty-two microprocessors," he boasted. When he pressed the rectangle below the monitor, a small keyboard popped out. The robot was equipped with its own minicomputer, which could connect to a computer and process information from the Internet, like the latest weather report.

"It will print out what you say to it and you can correct its mistakes." Dad pushed the keyboard back in its slot and gave the robot an approving pat on its side.

"Cool," I said. Mom's laugh sounded fake. Zumu still looked disapproving. Pablo had come out from under the sofa and approached Robot cautiously.

"Wait until you see the rest," Dad answered.

He showed me a button on the robot's back that activated a metronome, to use when I practiced the piano or violin. "See this?" Dad pointed to a little hole. "A pencil sharpener. This is a smoke detector. If the robot smells smoke, it will tell Celia to leave the house. It won't malfunction." Our smoke detectors sometimes went off unexpectedly. That always made Dad really mad.

Pablo came close and gingerly put out a paw to touch the robot. When Dad popped a metal detector out of the robot's base, he jumped back and growled, his tail all big.

Dad went on like one of those TV advertisements that always said, "Wait, there's more!"

My robot could help me with my homework, Dad told me. I could teach it songs. Eventually, he could program it to teach me Chinese.

At that, Zumu looked interested. She was always after me to take regular lessons. Dad always said he'd teach me, maybe later.

"I think we can get it to load the dishwasher, and it's designed to help you clean up your room. I put an extension on its right arm so it can reach your ceiling." Dad grinned. "I adapted it from an interactive model we're designing for recycling garbage left in landfills all over the world."

Oh, great, I thought. Dad kept on talking, very pleased with himself. "We may even get it to vacuum. And it will be your alarm clock."

"Is this my new baby-sitter?" I asked.

Zumu stared, plainly horrified. Mom jumped up to stack dessert plates we'd left on the dining room table.

Dad stopped smiling, eyeing Zumu uncomfortably. "It will certainly keep Celia safe when we're not here."

"Does that mean I can have friends over when you and Mom aren't home?"

"I don't think it's ready for *that* much responsibility,"

Mom called from the dining room, "But maybe we can teach it to French braid."

"Don't tell your friends about it," Dad warned. "Plenty of people would like to get their hands on my prototype. Fisher's outfit would kill to know what we're doing." Mr. Fisher's outfit was called Ultronics. He and Dad went to MIT together, and whenever Dad or Mr. Weissman mentioned him, they would say, "Can't trust the guy."

Mom came out of the kitchen and looked at Dad, shaking her head. "Now, Alex, Maeve and Jennifer won't be running to give Fisher the specs. I'm sure Celia will want to show it to them as soon as she can." She carried another stack of plates into the kitchen and quickly came back for cups and wineglasses. Looking at me, she said, "I really wish I could stay home all the time, Celia. But Calyx has to keep touring to stay alive. I'm flying to Winnipeg tomorrow, remember?"

Zumu stood up and followed Mom into the kitchen. "I can take care of this, Grace," Mom said to her. "I need something to keep my mind off all those concerts in Canada."

Mom always wanted Zumu to start home to Brookline early, and I knew she didn't really want Zumu to help her. Zumu has her own funny way of doing things, Mom says, because she grew up with servants.

Zumu is always amazed that Mom does everything without servants. Zumu's told me lots of stories about growing up in Shanghai. She had a live-in baby-sitter, called an amah, and she hardly ever saw her parents.

I hugged Zumu good-bye, and waved as she drove away. Then I went to the guest room to write a long e-mail to Grandmary and Grandpop.

After that, it was time for bed. While I put on my nightgown, Dad went to his workshop to get the recharger he'd rigged, a flat black platform that plugged into the outlet beside my bed. He shoved aside a pile of papers and puzzle boxes to make room for it. I led the robot from the living room to my bedroom, then snuggled down under the covers.

"Good night, Robot," I said.

"Good night, Celia." The robot rolled over the recharger and latched on. The blue light shining from its dome dimmed.

"It's charging now. It will automatically disconnect when it's fully recharged," Dad explained.

Standing in the doorway to my room, Dad tucked in his shirt and pushed his glasses up on his nose. He looked very proud of himself and his invention. "You've only seen a fraction of its capacity," he said. Typical Dad.

Slowly, he looked around my messy room. "I've programmed it to help you in many ways. Celia, this robot is going to change your life."

4

Changes Begin

It was strange. I was sitting at my school desk during some kind of music lesson, wondering why Maeve would rub a plastic jump rope handle over my arm. Then I woke up. Even though I'd been dreaming, the gentle plastic touch on my arm was real. So was the music, a bouncy synthesized version of "Twinkle, Twinkle, Little Star."

I rolled over, still bleary-eyed with sleep. A domed shape loomed over me, its blue light blinking slowly. Then I remembered the robot. It stood beside my bed, its "hand" on my arm. It must have disconnected itself from the recharger and rolled closer to my bed.

I rubbed my eyes and blinked. The music stopped, and the robot greeted me with a cheerful rhythm in its synthesized voice: "Good morning, Celia. Nice day, isn't it?"

The sky was gray, and raindrops slid down my window.

"It looks like a terrible day," I mumbled.

The robot answered in the same bouncy tone as before: "The weather may not be perfect. But you are up and ready to start an interesting day at school."

Then, somehow, its voice flattened: "Please put on your robe and slippers and join your parents for breakfast now."

Dad had said the robot would be my new alarm clock. I sure needed one, after sending that long e-mail to Grandmary and Grandpop last night. But Dad didn't tell me it would be giving orders.

I was wide awake now, so I rolled out of bed. I pulled my robe from the bottom of a heap of clothes on the floor. My slippers were harder to find. One was under my bed. I had to think for a minute before I remembered that the other one was stuffed behind some books on my bookshelf.

Mom's cello case and rolling travel bag leaned against the bench in the vestibule. She was already dressed in her traveling jeans and sweater. She hugged me, then poured me a cup of hot cocoa. "Just in time for breakfast," she said as I sat down beside Dad at the long counter.

I started my poached egg. It tasted delicious.

"How do you like your robot?" Dad asked.

"Is it going to wake me up every morning?"

"Not on weekends," Dad said, spreading a thin layer of marmalade on his toast. "But in general, it's programmed to perform some necessary functions."

I sipped my cocoa. It tasted better hot. Then I realized that was why the egg tasted better too. Long ago, Mom and Dad had given up trying to make me eat breakfast with them.

"What do you mean—functions?" I asked.

"You'll find out." Dad glanced at Mom.

She stared into her coffee cup. "It's meant to help." Mom paused. "If you let it."

That sounded a little ominous.

I had to admit, breakfast also tasted better when you weren't rushing to eat it. I went back to my room, thinking how much time I had and how I could read a bit before getting dressed or making my bed.

The robot had other ideas. It stood at the end of my bed, waiting for me. "Now is the time to make your bed." The synthesized voice sounded firm. "Please signify completion of task."

I'm not sure why I followed Robot's orders. Probably because it was new, and at that moment, the whole thing seemed like some kind of game.

Anyway, I pushed Pablo off the bed, pulled the sheets up, smoothed out my comforter, and arranged my stuffed animals.

"I've finished!" I sang out.

The robot wheeled around the bed. It smoothed the comforter with its right hand. Its globe eyes turned downward, and the blue light positively jumped with delight. That's how it learned what a made bed felt like, though I didn't know it then.

After beeping out a few bars of "Ode to Joy," the robot said: "Good work! It is most efficient to brush your teeth and wash your face before getting dressed. Please do so now."

I made a quick trip to the bathroom. I didn't stop to wonder why I was obeying a rolling plastic canister. It was like playing a video game. It didn't bother me then that I was doing the running around, not the little things on the screen. I wanted to see what the robot would do next.

I waved my hand in an arc before its globe eyes. "I'm back," I told it.

It played some happy melody—Mozart, I think—then spoke again: "At 7:14 A.M., it is time to get dressed."

The blouse Zumu gave me smelled new and felt crisp and smooth on my shoulders as I buttoned it. I slid the jumper over my head, but I couldn't reach the zipper.

Mom said the robot was meant to help. "Can you pull up my zipper?" I asked it. I was not sure it understood me, but I turned around anyway. If it could see an unmade bed, it must be able to tell that the back of my dress was wide open.

I felt it grasp the zipper and pull it.

"Thank you," I said in spite of myself. I was not all that surprised when it answered, "You're welcome."

I dug through the tangled underwear, ribbons, and tights in my top dresser drawer, searching for a pair of clean matching socks. Pablo pounced on my bare toes. I jumped from one foot to the other, teasing him. Then I threw a balled-up sock for him to chase. Pablo made me giggle so hard I'd forgotten all about the robot. But the robot hadn't forgotten about me. I was its job.

A shrill alarm bell almost made me jump out of my skin. It sounded like an ambulance. The camcorder eyes swiveled toward me. Bright lightning zapped out of the dome, and the synthesized voice shouted: *"Activity inappropriate to task! Cease immediately!"*

Pablo scuttered out of my room, his ears back, his tail down. I was so startled I plunked down on my bed and put on my socks and shoes.

The alarm noise stopped as suddenly as it started, and a soft, soothing melody began. The robot fairly chimed: "The time is 7:22 A.M."

I didn't feel like playing the game anymore. I was beginning to wish I'd never seen the robot. I sat on the bed, my feet flat on the floor, glaring at it.

It didn't notice my glare. Instead, it made its longest speech so far. "Now that you have finished dressing, it is time to collect the necessary articles for school. On Monday your class makes a regular visit to the library. Assuming the maximum borrowing privilege, you should return four books this week. Please locate them and the books you will need for school."

I sat there, determined not to move, wondering how it knew. What could those two moving globes see? The robot backed up, then extended a long hooked rod from its right arm, reaching for my feet.

Without thinking, I tucked my feet up under me. For one horrible moment I thought it was going to grab my ankle. But it fished under my bed and pulled out last year's backpack. A hole had frayed through the bottom, so I had stuffed it under the bed and forgotten about it.

Robot stood in front of me, the dusty old bag

dangling from the fingers on its right hand, its brown globes looking up at me—I swear—hopefully. It was so pitiful, I had to laugh.

"Wrong backpack," I said. "It's got a hole in it."

"Retrieved item not useful?" It did sound a bit plaintive.

"No!" I giggled.

It glided to the wastebasket and dropped my old bag in. The dome slowly rotated, and the eyes settled on my newer backpack, half filled, leaning against my dresser. Robot dragged it across the floor and pushed it between my feet.

What could I do?

One library book was under my bureau, another used as a tent for tiny horses to sleep under, the third weighed down a stack of papers. I dropped them in my backpack, one by one. Robot watched me and counted, "One, two, three."

The fourth book, *The Long Winter,* lay open beside my bed. I still had plenty of time, I thought. I stretched out, wondering if Laura would ever see spring. I opened the book just to read a page or two.

It is very hard to read with bells ringing and clanging, and lights flashing. Again I heard the synthesized shout: *"Activity inappropriate to task! Cease immediately!"* Then, in a quieter tone: "The time is 7:31 A.M. Please signify completion of task."

It was later than I thought. I dropped *The Long Winter,* my notebook, my pencils, and my good-luck bear into my backpack.

"I did it, you big fat domehead!" I yelled. I know it's stupid, but I suddenly had this irrational fear that the robot would scold me for being rude. But all it said was: "Starting for the school bus stop now will ensure a timely arrival. Do not forget your lunch and violin. Have a good day at school."

Just then the telephone rang. I picked up in Mom and Dad's bedroom and heard Jennifer's voice, asking Mom if she could speak to me. Jen wanted to know if I was wearing pants or a skirt to school. After describing my new jumper, I started to tell her about my morning with Robot, until Robot, in the hallway, began a very annoying rhythmic beep that made it impossible to talk.

"Gotta go," I said. "See you."

I grabbed my violin from the guest room, where Mom and I had been playing duets over the weekend, as I ran down the hall. I found Mom organizing food in the freezer. I could tell she was thinking about the concerts in Canada because her eyes were glazed over.

"Grandpop and Grandmary got your e-mail." She opened a drawer for waxed paper to wrap two cookies for my lunchbox. "Dad can open theirs when he gets home from work." She hugged me tight. "See you Friday. Take care of yourself and the robot." She put her hands on my shoulders and looked at me seriously. "Oh, Celia, I'm going to miss you. I wish I could be in two places at once." She gave me another hug and kiss.

Dad came down the hall, all combed and dressed for work. He handed me my umbrella and waved me off. He never kisses me good-bye. "See you around six," he said.

I walked down Heartwright Lane, listening to the raindrops drum against my umbrella. I splashed in the puddles and stopped to find a cardinal singing its rain song from the top of the Levins' maple tree.

It was the first time I'd arrived at the bus stop early since I started fifth grade.

When the bus came, I found a seat and looked through the window to see Tim O'Mara running along Woodland Road from the estate's old gatehouse, where he and his mom lived. Mrs. Flynt waited for him, and when he got on, she greeted him cheerfully.

He clomped down the aisle. His hair was all wet and messy. He moved to sit down next to me, but I pushed my backpack in the way. "This seat is saved!" I told him. As if I'd let him sit in Maeve's place!

"Saved for an ugly dog." The second graders in the seat across looked a little frightened as he thumped past them down the aisle.

Mrs. Flynt looked at us in her rearview mirror. "We don't call names, Tim," she said calmly. I was waiting for the day Mrs. Flynt would throw Tim off the bus for bothering me, but all she ever did was bawl him out a little. How could she be so nice to that stupid jerk?

5

Robot Helps Out

A cold, damp wind blew gray-edged clouds across the sky as I walked slowly up Heartwright Lane after school. By the time I reached our front walk, Tim was heading up the hill. I forgot Mom was on tour, so I tried the door. Locked. I stood there, cold and lonely, dreading the dark house. I stared up at the estate house, trying to remember the code for disabling Dad's security system. In the distance I could see Tim looking down at me. Shivering, I turned away and shrugged off my backpack. As I dug down, trying to find the scrap of paper Dad used to write the new code, the front door swung open. In the lighted, warm vestibule, Robot stood waiting for me.

"Wow!" Tim's yell floated down from the hill. He must have seen Robot! I rushed into the house and slammed the door.

Inside, I smiled at Robot, feeling a little silly for being so grateful to a plastic canister because it opened the door. Robot sounded almost sincere when it said, "Welcome home, Celia." It rolled up to the wall console that controlled

Dad's fancy security system and spoke to it in clicks and beeps. Then it asked, "Did you have a good day at school?"

"Yes, but I have a lot of homework." I wondered how much I could trust Robot. In the end it didn't matter. I had to tell someone, and Pablo was probably asleep in the basement. I spoke to Robot the way Dad told me, the same way I spoke to Pablo when I was trying to make him understand. Slowly and with lots of expression.

"Mrs. Flower gave me ten extra math problems because I talked too much. I was telling my friends about you. They can't wait to see you."

It was spooky. Robot responded as if it understood. "Extra math problems to solve?"

"Yes," I said. I couldn't believe I was having a conversation with a robot.

"Do not worry. I am programmed to assist with math problems."

I shrugged off my coat, dropped my backpack, and started toward the kitchen, planning to let Pablo out of the basement and find something to eat.

Robot glided in front of me, its blue light pulsing, looking cross-eyed at the heap of clothes in the hall. "Please store outerwear properly before starting indoor activities," it reminded me.

I answered with a big, displeased sigh, but I hung up my coat and opened my umbrella to dry. I knew I should do that every day.

Robot waited in the kitchen while I opened the basement door so that Pablo could come up when he was ready. It watched me while I ate a banana and drank a glass of milk. When I slipped down from the stool and headed for my bedroom, Robot blocked my way again.

"Please dispose of garbage and put used glassware in dishwasher." Another thing I knew I should do every day but usually left for someone else. When I finished, it still blocked my way. I know I could have slipped around it, but I was curious. Now what did it want?

"Let us enter a few important items into my memory bank. Please retrieve backpack."

I hauled my backpack up on the counter and dug down to find the things Robot kept asking for. Eventually, I found my Suzuki class schedule scrunched at the bottom, where it had been since Mrs. Eastman had handed it out on the third day of school. The library books were easier; they were on top. I had renewed *The Long Winter*. It took me a while to remember that I'd stuck the lists of dates for book reports and tests in spelling, math, and French on my bedroom bulletin board. Dad had told me to write all those dates on my calendar, but I never did. Later I covered the schedules with a picture of a Siamese cat growling at four monkeys and forgot all about them.

Robot followed me down to my room, where it waited patiently as I gathered the schedules. I read aloud my list of assignments and due dates slowly and clearly. After each one, Robot beeped, then said, "Entered. Next, please?" When we had finished, it said, "Thank you. Now I will be able to remind you on appropriate occasions."

I pulled *The Long Winter* from my stack of library

books. I still wondered if Laura would ever see spring. Robot, determined to be annoying, played "Whistle While You Work" in such a steady rhythm that I couldn't even read a line. I slammed the book shut.

"Time to do your homework," Robot repeated, just as cheerfully. "You will find it easier with my assistance." It almost sounded comforting. "Have you started the book report that is due tomorrow?"

"I'm working on it now, Plastic Pea-brain," I said. "But I have to finish this book first." I waved *The Long Winter* in front of the globe eyes.

"Signify completion of activity," Robot answered calmly, and I thought it looked understanding. It stood perfectly still, its hum a soft whisper, while I curled up on my bed to read. Pablo entered my bedroom warily, keeping his distance from Robot. Eventually he jumped onto my bed.

"Spring came!" I told Robot. "Laura woke up in the middle of the night and smelled it. That was a good book." You may think I was crazy, talking to a robot, but it was better than talking to myself, which sometimes I do, though I hate to admit it. I'm not really nutty, just alone a lot.

"Now that input is completed, output may commence," Robot observed. I knew it meant I should start my book report. Dad talked like that sometimes. I sprawled on the floor in front of my laptop.

"Remember the elementary principles of composition," Robot recited in its beeping monotone. "One. Choose a suitable design. Two. Make the paragraph the unit of composition. Three. Use the active voice. . . ."

It continued while I sat up and glared at it. "I can't think while you're talking, and besides, I don't need your advice. I always get stars on my book reports." It ignored me completely and kept droning. Its last words were: "Reading passages aloud to me will enhance my understanding. I will monitor spell-check execution."

"My spell-check works fine, Domehead," I told it. "Now shut up and let me write." It actually kept quiet as I worked, and it listened as I read aloud to it. After I finished and ran the spell-check, the red light glowed from its chest. The infrared light must be beaming data. Robot was up to something.

"Passages read aloud to enhance voice recognition will be displayed on the computer screen. Later corrections will improve my skill," Robot said. "Misspelled words are entered in my memory," it added. "Now I can help you learn the proper spellings." That was anything but reassuring.

I pushed a pile of clean T-shirts off the printer and pulled it out from under my desk. Sure enough, when I printed out my book report, a list of the words I'd originally misspelled followed. I pinned the list on my bulletin board, thinking a spell-check was easier.

"Computer is not sited for optimal user comfort," Robot remarked.

It was right. I did feel stiff and sore after lying on my stomach so long.

"I took Dad's old MindMate apart on my desk," I explained. "I got stuck and I can't put it back together.

Dad hasn't had time to help me." The MindMate was a really old computer of Dad's.

"I have a MindMate manual logged in my memory bank," Robot said. "I can provide information and assistance for reassembly."

"You can?" For one short moment of excitement, I was totally happy to have Robot. I was ready to start right then, but naturally Robot had other ideas.

"I am unable to release discretionary information until required assignments are completed," it told me. I might have known it would make me finish my homework first.

"Please locate math problem sheet and sharpened pencil." I dug my arithmetic book, where I'd stuffed the problem sheets, out of my backpack.

"I don't have a sharp pencil." Mom or Dad would have told me not to sulk, but Robot didn't seem to notice.

"You may use the hole in my back to sharpen pencils."

There was a handful of dull pencils in my top desk drawer. I picked one up and stuck it in the hole. I felt it vibrate gently, heard a soft whir, and saw an amber light.

"Wow!" I said to the fine point, echoing Tim. I settled on my bed with an old picture book as a lap desk. Robot glided near.

"I compute more efficiently than your calculator. You are welcome to make use of my keyboard."

The keyboard slid out from under Robot's monitor, and I whipped through the ten extra problems in the time it usually took me to do two. Then it hit me. I'd been home from school just over an hour, and I'd done all my homework. Usually I was arguing with Dad or Mom that I had to stay up past bedtime to finish.

I folded my problem sheet neatly, stuck it back in my arithmetic book, and stood over my desk. "Now, about that MindMate. MindMate," I repeated the key word clearly, to make sure Robot understood.

Robot had other ideas. "Tomorrow you have a piano lesson. Practice is essential to master an instrument. I will follow you to the piano to help with tempo."

Someday, I thought as I marched and Robot rolled down the hall to the living room, someday I'm going to figure out how to reprogram that hunk of plastic to do what I want. The music for "Für Elise" lay open on the piano. I had tried it once last week, and it sounded pretty awful. As I took my seat on the piano bench, I heard a rhythmic click. Robot explained: "Metronome activated." The keyboard slid out again. "Please use keyboard to indicate desired tempo."

Mrs. Kershaw would never believe this.

I set a very slow tempo to make things easier. Having Robot as my metronome made practicing more fun, so I played longer than I usually did. The notes seemed like golden stairs, leading me up and down, slowly at first, then more quickly after I reset Robot's metronome. I was still practicing when Dad came home.

"Well, what do you think of the robot?" Dad asked me as we sat at the counter in the kitchen, digging our chopsticks into Chinese food he'd brought from Omei.

Omei is the Chinese restaurant next to the building where that awful Christian Fisher works.

"It's very bossy, but it did help me out. I finished my homework." As I told him that, I realized he hadn't asked me about my homework when he came in the door, the way he usually did.

Dad smiled and spooned more chicken and cashews into my rice bowl.

"Does it really have a MindMate manual in its memory bank?"

"Yes. And a great graphics program. It'll diagram step by step. It should be good at sorting things, too. Ask it to help you clean out a drawer sometime."

"Not tonight, okay? I haven't read Grandmary's e-mail yet, and I want to work on the MindMate."

"How about doing some voice recognition work?"

"I read to it already while I was writing my book report."

Mom or my teachers would have praised me, but Dad usually didn't. All he said was, "Let's take a few minutes to look it over after the dishes are done."

When Mom wasn't home, it was my job to clean up the kitchen.

"Think Robot could feed the dishwasher?" I asked.

"Let's see. You'll have to show it how."

"Robot!" I called.

I heard it roll across the floor. Soon it glided into the kitchen and stopped in front of me. "Let's clear the table," I told it. "Watch me."

I opened the dishwasher and positioned my rice bowl on the top shelf. Robot's camcorder eyes swiveled to follow my hands, and the blue light between them blinked faster. It stood just above the level of the counter.

"Here, you do it." I handed Robot Dad's rice bowl. The articulated fingers grasped it delicately, and then carefully set it next to mine.

I clapped my hands, giving it the praise I had wanted. "Good work!" I shouted. With a little more instruction, Robot lined up the plates on the bottom shelf and put our plastic chopsticks in the basket. When we were done, it reminded me to make my lunch before Dad finished the dishes.

Dad looked over the passages I had read aloud to Robot and used its keyboard to correct a few words it didn't understand. Before disappearing into his workshop, he booted up Mom's computer in the TV room so that I could read Grandmary's e-mail. I couldn't boot it up myself because Dad didn't let me have Internet access when I was home alone.

I still had time to work on the MindMate. First I scooped up the pieces of the radio on my desk and dumped them on the floor to get them out of the way. Dad was right. Robot was a whiz at graphics. Each step was diagrammed on its screen, so I was able to get the thing running before I went to bed. When I was finished, Robot reminded me to clean up all the scraps and bits of metal and plastic. The MindMate stood whole on a perfectly clean desk.

"Tomorrow will be sunny, with a high of fifty-nine degrees Fahrenheit. Please lay out appropriate clothing." Robot sounded encouraging.

I draped a pair of jeans, a shirt, and a sweater over the top of the easel.

"For school tomorrow you will need the following items. Please place each item in your backpack as it is mentioned. One: Book and book report. One: Book and book report."

It kept repeating like a broken record while I looked for *The Long Winter*. Finally I found it on the floor under the far side of my bed, on top of a stack of old puzzles. I dug under a pile of papers on my dresser to find a folder for the book report.

"Two. Completed arithmetic problems." That was easy. They were on my bed.

"Three. Piano music." The music for "Für Elise" was still in the living room, so I ran to get it.

Amazing! My clothes were laid out, my schoolbag packed, the MindMate together, and there was still time to start a new library book before Dad came in to say good night. As I got into my nightgown, Robot backed into its recharger.

Mom had left me in the middle of *The Two Towers,* but I'd promised not to read ahead until she got back. Remembering her calm voice and the songs she sometimes sang after she turned out the lights made my throat ache and my eyes sting. To distract myself, I opened a book Mrs. Heins, the school librarian, had given me. She said it was really old, but she thought I'd like it: *Andy Buckram's Tin Men*. I did, because it was about this boy who owned robots. But it was kind of old-fashioned. Pablo settled in beside me. He was less afraid of Robot now.

"What are you going to do with that dinosaur?" Dad asked when he came in to turn out my lights. He meant the MindMate.

I hadn't thought what I'd do with it once I got it back together. I had my laptop, which was much better at word processing, and I could get on line with Mom's computer when Dad was home. That MindMate was designed long ago just for word processing.

"I don't know," I said. "Take it apart again?"

"Maybe later," Dad said quickly. "I'll put it in the basement for now. You will find this robot is able to do a lot more than help reassemble old computers."

Dad lugged the MindMate out of my room, but I really didn't care. I still had some locks and the radio to work on. And this weekend Mom would be home and I could invite Jennifer and Maeve to see Robot. As I drifted off to sleep in the familiar dark, I could see the blue light glowing through the dome, throbbing slowly.

Good night, sleep well, it seemed to say, over and over.

6

Dad Was Right

Robot did change my life, starting that first week. I didn't always like it, because it was so strict about making me do my homework, *and* practice my violin or piano, sometimes both, every day. On Tuesday Mrs. Kershaw told Dad how well I played Beethoven, and how I must have practiced all weekend. I didn't tell her that I'd only practiced once with Robot. In the car, Dad gave me a thumbs-up and said, *"Ding hao!"* which means "very good" in Chinese. I felt so happy.

After homework and practicing were done, Robot only wanted to do two things: listen to me read aloud and help me clean up. It displayed the words I read on its little monitor, and I used the keyboard to correct the ones it had misunderstood. I liked having it listen to me so much that I started talking to it as if it understood. It got better and better at answering back, so I began to think of it as a peculiar but helpful friend. Since I had more in common with it than Mrs. Boyer, I kind of forgot it was a machine. I wasn't alone with Pablo anymore. Sometimes I could even get it to play a game, like Trivial Questions.

I could also see that I was going to be spending more time with Robot than with Dad.

Every night after dinner, Robot and I worked on cleanup. By Wednesday my laptop and printer were back on my desk, so my room looked tidier. I kept finding odd things, like a photo from Aunt Susan and Uncle Eric's wedding. They stood in front, with both their families lined up around them. Mom and Dad and I were there in the front row with Zumu and Aunt Gail, smiling in the sunshine.

I held up the picture in front of Robot's eyes.

"See how different we look?" Zumu, Dad, and my aunts Susan and Gail were Chinese. Uncle Eric and his family were white, like my mom. I was half and half.

"More same than different," Robot said. It actually sounded like it was trying to comfort me. But I still thought we all looked like pieces of two puzzles that didn't quite match.

Thinking about puzzles reminded me of the old portable radio. That was one puzzle I could solve.

I moved my laptop aside and sorted the radio pieces on my desk. Dad was locked in his workshop, so Robot helped me assemble the pieces. If I hadn't been missing one transistor, I could have made the radio work. Since Robot was so determined to clean up my room, I knew we would find that missing transistor eventually.

Tuesday morning when Tim got on the bus, he perched beside me instead of going to his seat in the back.

"That's some cool toy you got for your birthday," he said.

"It's not a toy. And you're in Maeve's seat," I answered.

"Can I come and see—"

"No!" He was so annoying. "Get out of Maeve's seat!"

Tim hadn't always been so obnoxious. When I started kindergarten, he used to sit next to me on the bus and walk me home. He was a lot nicer to me then, like a big brother. He's a year older than me, and I thought he was so smart and wise. After I'd been in school awhile, and got to be friends with Maeve, she told me girls couldn't be friends with boys. That was after Tim kept bugging us on the bus, trying to butt into our conversations.

Tim got up, but not before "accidentally" turning my backpack upside down on the floor. My books fell out, and my good-luck bear slid under the seat in front of me. I was still putting stuff back when the bus got to Maeve's stop.

News of my robot spread around Abigail Adams. Kids were always asking me about it, wondering when I would bring it to school. I felt more conspicuous than ever, and almost wished I'd never mentioned my birthday present. A hot shiver of guilt ran up my chest when I thought how Dad would feel if he knew how many kids were talking about Robot.

He didn't even know that Tim had seen Robot.

"What's Tim doing up there in the carriage house?" Dad asked on Thursday. He came home before dark that night, hoping to test the No Dogs button, but it was raining. He'd seen Tim standing with Rocky and Mark in the lighted doorway of the estate's carriage house. Dad didn't usually notice anything that went on outside his workshop, so I explained about Tim working for Mark Ludlow.

"He should be home studying," Dad said. "He's wasting time up there." I didn't answer, because I didn't care what Tim did with his time, as long as he didn't bother me.

By Friday, I'd gotten so used to having the door open as soon as I reached the house that I didn't even look for my key. When the door opened, I was surprised to see Dad standing in the lighted vestibule, looking very pleased with himself. I smelled fresh-baked cookies. Dad reminded me to hang up my coat just as I was starting to do it.

"Where's Mom?" I asked. "And Robot?"

Mom came out of the kitchen, smiling at me. She hugged me tight. She'd changed into her jeans, but her hair still smelled like an airplane. "We left Toronto early because they'd mixed up a booking." She twisted back her hair. "Dad came home to meet the Calyx van. After all that confusion, I felt like baking cookies."

I sat down at the counter to wolf down cookies and milk while Dad stood in the kitchen doorway, nibbling one cookie. Mom sounded excited and proud when she said, "Your room looks great! Your bed's even made. You must have had a busy week with Robot."

"It sure is bossy," I answered.

"At least you don't have paint on your sweater," she teased. "Have you started on your closet yet?"

"Not yet, but Robot used its extension arm to reach every sock I ever threw up into the globe light. It's cool the way its wrist bends."

"So that's why your room is so much brighter." Mom almost laughed as she scrubbed potatoes.

Dad grinned with pride. Pride for me, or for his creation? "Tell Mom what you taught it," he said.

"I taught it to make my bed and sing 'You Are My Sunshine.' It doesn't have much expression, but it can carry a tune. Dad thinks you can teach it to braid my hair."

Mom put the potatoes she'd been washing in the oven, along with stew from the freezer. "Dad has another job for you and Robot right now," she said. She gave Dad an amused, almost mischievous, smile. "They've been very busy in your room."

"I ran a test of its sorting capacity." Dad pushed his glasses against his nose. He looked a little nervous.

When I went to my room, I saw that my easel and beanbag chair were out in the hall. I couldn't walk across the floor of my room, because everything I'd stuffed under my bed, plus junk that must have come from under my dresser and the bottom dresser drawer, was arranged in neat piles on my floor. Old puzzle boxes were in one pile, sheets of paper were in another, and pencils, crayons, markers, puzzle pieces, assorted Lego blocks, doll shoes, old socks, and bits of metal that were obviously part of a lock all had their own piles, too. There was also the missing transistor from my radio, and a box with ten silver dollars that Zumu gave me after her trip to Las Vegas. Pablo walked cautiously around the edge, sniffing the different piles.

"Robot will tell you what to do," Dad said, and headed off to his workshop.

In the TV room, Mom sorted through mail while the potatoes roasted and the stew warmed up. Even though Mom and Dad were both in the house, I felt like I was still alone with Robot.

It gave me orders in its flat synthesized voice. "First, discard outmoded or unusable items. Second, put away items belonging elsewhere. Third, arrange remaining items for easy retrieval in storage space."

It was the last thing I wanted to do on a Friday afternoon. But I couldn't walk across the floor. And Pablo would start playing with all the little things very soon, making a bigger mess. Also, I knew Robot wouldn't do anything else until I finished.

The socks were way too small, so I pitched them in the wastebasket. Then I stood on a chair to put shoes on the barefooted dolls sitting on top of my bookcase, sharpened the pencils in Robot's back hole and put them in a big cup on my desk, and put away the Lego blocks. I did my best to figure out where each puzzle piece belonged and add it the right box. When I held a silver dollar on my palm to admire and polish with my finger, Robot started its impatient noises, so I tucked the box under my underwear in my tidy top dresser drawer.

"Wow!" Mom exclaimed, standing in my doorway.

"You and that robot have worked hard!" She turned away, then added over her shoulder, "Dinner in about half an hour."

I had to admit, it was more fun cleaning with Robot than with Mom. We would get into big arguments about what should be thrown away. I always got a headache and she always went off for a long practice, the kind I didn't dare interrupt. I usually ended up by stuffing everything back where it was. Now I could take my time deciding what to throw away. I surprised myself by pitching a lot.

Finally, I opened up the radio, popped in the missing transistor, plugged it in, and turned it on. Out came a blast of sound: some DJ shouting. I was amazed at how good I felt. It wasn't just the radio. With my room clean, I felt like I was looking out from a mountaintop instead of hacking through a tangled jungle. Still, I had to wonder: Did Dad think all I was good for was testing a robot?

I found Mom in the dining room, putting place mats and napkins on the table. She handed me some cutlery. While I laid out knives, forks, and spoons the way Grandmary had taught me, I said, "Can Maeve and Jennifer come over this weekend? They're dying to see Robot."

"Sunday we're going for dim sum with Zumu, so it'll have to be tomorrow." Dim sum is a Chinese brunch you always eat in a restaurant. Sometimes you sit there for hours. Mom added plaintively, "Maybe next weekend you'll get to the closet?"

I phoned Maeve and Jen right away.

Mom and Dad started dinner in a good mood. Dad

was happy that Robot had been able to tell the difference between Lego blocks and the pieces of the lock. It didn't seem like a big deal to me. Mom was happy because she'd gotten a letter from someone at MIT that confirmed arrangements for her solo concert next January.

Dad lifted his wineglass. "Here's to your recital," he said.

"I wish my mother and father could be there." Mom stared at the candle.

"You'll be great," Dad answered vaguely. He was the one who had urged her to plan a solo recital and found out whom to contact at MIT, but tonight he had other things on his mind. Dad didn't seem to notice, but when Mom's mood changed so quickly from happy to sad I always felt a little bit scared. That night I felt a prickling along my spine that made me think of Pablo when his fur stood up.

To change the subject, I announced, "Maeve and Jen can both come over tomorrow. They can't wait to see Robot."

"I didn't know about this," Dad said ominously. "When?"

"In the morning. Maeve has to be home in the afternoon. Her uncle's coming."

"I need to go grocery shopping," Mom said to Dad, "but you'll be home to supervise."

Dad looked annoyed. "Can't you go shopping in the afternoon? I have to be at the lab all day tomorrow, to go over the robot's enhanced capacities with Caleb." Mr.

Weissman had an apartment, but he seemed to live in his office at Moria Systems.

"Nature's Bounty is such a zoo on Saturday afternoons," Mom said.

I pushed my food around on my plate. Dad could get really irritated when he couldn't go ahead with plans he'd made. Their good mood had already turned sour and I was afraid they'd start yelling.

"Go to the Food Mart, then." Dad's voice already had an irritated edge. Food Mart was a chain store in East Haven. Dad often stopped there for fruit on his way home from work. "Why are you so stubborn?"

Mom tucked her hair behind her ear, pressed her lips together, and stood up abruptly to toss the salad. "I just think the food is healthier at Nature's Bounty. I'll go shopping tomorrow afternoon, after Maeve and Jen leave. Celia can come with me if she wants."

"I guess it will be all right," Dad said. I thought he meant it would be all right for Maeve and Jennifer to come over, but later I realized he meant it would be all right if they saw Robot.

7

Robot Learns to French Braid

Saturday morning I woke up by myself. Robot sat on its charger, its blue light softly throbbing. I guessed we would both sleep late on weekends. My robe hung over my bed, my slippers sat on the floor. I put them on and went down to the kitchen, where I found Mom and Dad chatting comfortably over the remains of their breakfast.

Mom smoothed down my hair. "Celia, after your breakfast, how would you like to let me try to teach Robot to French braid your hair? Dad wants to see this before he goes off to work."

So there we were, in my bathroom, with me looking in the mirror while Mom and Robot stood behind me on each side. Dad leaned against the doorway, watching. Mom got out two combs and put one in Robot's left pincher hand. She divided my hair in half, and she combed one side, while Robot, its camcorder eyes googling around, combed the other.

That felt really weird.

"Don't let the comb touch the skin on my head," I told it. "Pull it gently through the hair."

"Action could cause discomfort?" Robot asked.

"That's right." Mom and I spoke together, but Robot only heard me.

"I am programmed not to cause discomfort or harm," it answered.

Once they had combed my hair, Mom showed Robot how to separate three strands, still using the comb in its pincher hand. She demonstrated, then guided its fingers to plait the three strands together. I couldn't see what they were doing, but I felt a sharp pull on Robot's side.

"Ouch!" I cried.

"Action caused discomfort?"

"It's all right, you're just learning." It had sounded so apologetic, I couldn't help trying to soothe its feelings, even though I knew it didn't really have any feelings. "Just don't pull so hard."

"Technique assimilated," it replied.

Mom finished braiding and tied up her side with an elastic band. "Robot did a great job," she said. "When I'm not here, it should be able to braid both sides."

In the mirror, I could see Dad grinning proudly and raising his thumb in a gesture that meant *"Ding hao!"*

"Good job!" I said to Robot. It piped a few bars of "Ode to Joy." And my braids were set for the weekend.

When Jennifer and Maeve came into the vestibule, I asked, "Like my braids?" and turned around to show them.

"One side's tighter than the other," Maeve said.

"Robot did that side," I explained, flipping Robot's braid forward. "It's still learning."

"Your braids look great," Jen said as I led them to my room. She had brought her flute in its case and a stuffed dog from her collection. "Wow," she said, "and your room is so much neater!"

My two best friends are totally different. Jennifer always looks pulled together. Her hair is a pretty brown, and it's always combed into a smooth ponytail. She doesn't know as many things as Maeve and I do, but she remembers things about people. She knows I get lonely when Mom is gone and she always calls to cheer me up. The first weeks of school, she had called me nearly every morning to find out what I was going to wear. After Robot came, she called me every night to ask what I had laid out and what we'd had for dinner.

Maeve is really smart, with a huge vocabulary, and when she's in a good mood, she can think up the most amazing stories for us to play. She and Jen were friends before we all met in kindergarten, so she doesn't mind that Jen and I are friends now. Sometimes she can be really nasty, though, especially when she thinks Jen or I like someone better than her. Also, I think she wishes she didn't have so many freckles, that her hair wasn't so wild and red, and that she was skinny and coordinated like Jen.

Maeve gently placed her big teddy bear on my smooth bedspread. She always treated the bear like it was alive. When I introduced Robot, Maeve and Jen seemed a little disappointed. I think they expected it to look more like a human being. They couldn't understand why it could hear me and not them. At first, I didn't let them use the remote, because Dad had told me not to.

Still, they were pretty impressed when it gave them the weather forecast for the next several days. "We don't have to put away our sandals just yet," Jen said when she heard how warm it would be. Maeve went wild writing out stupendous columns of figures. She and Jen were amazed by how quickly Robot added them up.

After he got used to the idea that my friends would see Robot, Dad had suggested that we play a matching game with the stuffed animals. He left long before they arrived, so he wasn't there to watch Robot examine Maeve's big bear with its globe eyes.

The blue light pulsed as I said, "That is a teddy bear. Turn toward my bookcase. Can you find another teddy bear?"

We three watched silently as Robot wheeled toward my bookcase and focused on the dolls and stuffed toys crammed together on the top shelf. Methodically, it reached out its extension arm to grab the toys, one by one, passing them close to its globe eyes and pulsing blue light. Jen giggled to see it look so cross-eyed and concentrated. It found all three of my teddy bears and lined them up neatly beside Maeve's.

"Good work!" I cried out, clapping my hands. "You found all the bears!"

Robot used the same technique to pair two stuffed rabbits with floppy ears, three pigs, and a stuffed cat and dog, probably because they both had long legs and small ears. That one mistake started us all giggling.

"No, Robot," I said. "This is a cat. Like Pablo." I pushed its articulated plastic fingers, showing it how to grasp the stuffed cat by the scruff of the neck. "Look at it." Robot did.

Then I took away the cat and held out the dog. Robot grabbed its back. "And this is a dog."

"Information assimilated," Robot answered, which made us laugh some more.

Then Jennifer played her flute along with Robot's metronome. I showed Robot how to dance with Maeve's teddy bear. It put out its hose arms, gripped the teddy bear's top legs with two of its left-hand pinchers, and circled around to its own synthesized version of "Blue Danube." That made us laugh until we were all breathless. Then Maeve said, "Let's play something."

Jen called out, "Trivial Questions, with teams!" She knew I played with Robot. "Dibs! The robot's my partner," she added quickly.

"No fair!" Maeve cried.

I thought quickly. Mom had closed the door to the guest room, where she was learning the cello part of a modern sonata for her recital. The music marched on for a few notes, then stopped and repeated. Mom had probably forgotten all about us.

"Let's take Robot outside," I said. "We can see how well the No Dogs button works." The sun had come out after a week of wet weather, so I knew it would be safe to take Robot out.

Jen made a face, and to keep her from arguing, I handed her Robot's remote control and showed her how to walk it down the hall. "We've got to be quiet," I said, "so we won't disturb Mom."

We followed Robot down the hall, past the closed door. I didn't tell Maeve and Jen that I was pretty sure Mom wouldn't let me take Robot outside if I asked, but I really wanted to show Maeve and Jen what it could do.

We crossed Heartwright Lane and went closer to the iron fence than I had ever dared before. Rocky came running so fast that I didn't think to look up the hill for Mark Ludlow. We all took a step back when Rocky reached the fence, barking and growling at us, showing his huge white teeth. I waited a minute while he got all worked up, then pressed the No Dogs button. He stood still for a minute, then ran away, whining, his ears back, his tail between his legs. Mark Ludlow came running down the hill, calling, "Here boy!"

I turned to Maeve and Jen, feeling triumphant. "See how Robot can scare a dog?"

Jen chuckled at Rocky's defeat, but Maeve stared up at the estate house. "What's Tim O'Mara doing up there, and who's that with him?" she asked. Tim watched us from the upper edge of the mansion's lawn, where he had been cutting brush. Another man, stooped and pale, stood behind him, holding clippers, wearing loose, grungy clothes and a dark blue knitted cap. A long stringy ponytail fell from underneath the cap and down his back.

"Tim helps Mark Ludlow sometimes. I've never seen

the other guy before." Dad sometimes complained that Mrs. Prentice spent so much time in Florida that she didn't know what was going on in her own house.

Mark fastened Rocky's collar to a leash and started toward us. "Get away from the fence!" he yelled. "Don't bother my dog!"

I wasn't afraid of him, but I was worried Mom would hear all the commotion. Dad would be really mad at me if he knew that a stranger had seen Robot.

"Come on, let's go," I said. Jen handed Maeve the remote control, and we all went back inside and collapsed on the living room sofa. Jen and I laughed helplessly as Maeve imitated Mark: "'Don't bother my dog.' What nerve!" Robot stood beside the sofa, with its eyes relaxed and its blue dome glowing softly.

"Hey, Maeve," Jen said, trying to catch her breath between giggles, "did you see how Tim looked at Celia? I think he likes her."

Maeve started to sing, "Tim and Celia sitting in a tree, K-I-S-S—"

I hit Maeve with a pillow to make her stop. She used to tease me about Tim a lot more when we were younger, until he got so pesty and mean that I stopped speaking to him. I said, "He just wanted a good look at Robot! We hate each other and you know it."

"Cool it, Celia." Jen stood up and turned on the stereo on the bookshelf. "Tim's just a big, dumb nobody." The station was set to FM classical, but it didn't take her long to find a pop music station. "Want to come to my house for Halloween? We can have dinner and then go trick-or-treating."

Jen lived in an old development, where the houses were close together and people loved to see kids in costume. We hardly had any trick-or-treaters in our neighborhood.

When Mom came to tell us it was almost time for Jen and Maeve to go, I asked her, "Will you be home this Halloween?"

"I will," she answered, "so plan on doughnuts after trick-or-treating." Jen gestured thumbs up. She loved Mom's homemade doughnuts.

"What are you going to be?" Maeve asked Jennifer as we went to my room to get Jen's flute and stuffed dog and Maeve's teddy bear. Robot wheeled after us.

"A princess. What about you?"

"Mama bear, and my bear will be my baby. What are you going to be, Celia?"

"I don't know yet," I said.

"Why don't you be a robot?" Maeve said, looking at Robot backing into its charger. "You could cover a cardboard box with foil."

"That's not a bad idea." I smiled, because I had an even better idea. I would go as a scientist, and I would take Robot out with me as my invention. I could even teach it to say, "Trick or treat."

8

Robot's Halloween

"Celia, where do you get these crazy ideas?" Dad slammed his newspaper down on the glass coffee table. "That robot's a valuable prototype, not some toy you can drag from house to house."

"Come on, Dad, it wouldn't get hurt. I'd be really careful. And it would be the best Halloween costume ever!"

"You know it can't climb stairs." When Dad gives these warnings, he always sounds like he's predicting the end of the world.

"It won't have to. Jen and Maeve can ring doorbells. I'll wait on the sidewalk. And Jen's house doesn't have a front porch, remember?"

"It'll be damaged if it gets mud on its wheels."

"Dad, I'll be really careful." Sometimes you have to say things more than once to get Dad to hear them. "There'll be sidewalks everywhere we go. I promise I'll keep it away from mud."

"Celia, you can't drag my invention out for everyone to see! What if some other computer scientist happens to see it? He'd know right away it's not a toy."

I had no logical answer for that, so I shouted, "It's *my* robot! You gave it to me for my birthday, remember? Why are you being so mean? All I want is to take it trick-or-treating with me! Besides, there aren't any computer scientists in Jen's neighborhood."

Mom stood in the living room with her hands on her hips. "Stop shouting, both of you! Time out, for heaven's sake. Alex, we go through this every year. You never went trick-or-treating, so you don't realize how important it is to Celia."

Dad moved to America from Taiwan when he was nine. He grew up in Brookline, and I've often heard how his father wouldn't let him go trick-or-treating. He's always nervous on Halloween night. He doesn't like strangers coming to the door, even the few who come to our neighborhood. When she was a little girl, Mom loved dressing up. She still wears a costume on Halloween to greet the few kids who might come to our house. Tim shows up every year for her doughnuts.

Dad started to snap back at Mom, but she sliced her hand across the air to cut him off.

"Would you both just listen? Celia, you've got to accept how Dad feels about that robot. It's true he gave you his prototype, but the robotics ideas really belong to him. So I have a compromise." She looked at Dad. "Why don't you and Celia make an imitation robot out of cardboard or something? She can take that with her."

"Maeve thought I should go as a robot, but if you helped me make a fake one it would be so cool," I told Dad.

Dad leaned back on the sofa and gave his glasses a one-finger push. "Not a bad idea," he said. "Let's start after dinner."

I hugged him, and Mom smiled.

Dad was off in his own world during dinner. Turned out he was planning a design for my Halloween robot. I wished he would discuss his ideas with me and let me help him plan. Dad was thinking so hard, he didn't hear Mom talking about her tour and telling me how many different kinds of people lived in Toronto.

"There are so many Chinese that a lot of the older ones can get along without learning English," she said.

I thought I would like to be in a crowd of people who looked like me, instead of being the only Asian kid in my school. Somehow, that made me think of Tim.

"Why does Tim have to be the only other kid in our neighborhood?" I asked.

"Don't you remember how you used to play with him when we first moved here?" Mom smiled at me. "You even invited him to your fourth birthday party. Dad hadn't built his workshop then, so he kept all his computer stuff in the TV room. Dad found Tim there while the rest of us were playing musical chairs, and told him off. He wanted to send Tim home, but you wouldn't let him."

I rolled my eyes. "Don't remind me," I said. "I was such a baby, I didn't know anything." I thought Tim was so cool then. Mom told me he came over dressed as a pirate the first Halloween we moved to West Haven. I don't remember that, but I do remember that he showed me how to throw a baseball and swing a bat. He even gave me a Red Sox baseball cap for the birthday that Mom was talking about. It was somewhere in my closet.

I felt sorry for Tim, too, because Mom told me his dad had been killed fighting a fire. Like all little kids, I thought firemen were pretty special. Then I got older and went to school and made friends with Maeve and Jen, and that's when Tim started to become a huge pest.

When we finished eating, Dad stood up. "Come on, Celia. Let's get started."

Dad hardly ever invited me into his workroom, so I didn't mind skipping dessert. All sorts of interesting stuff littered his workbenches: computer monitors; circuit boards looking like miniature cities, soldering irons, resin, bolts, nuts, wires of all colors and sizes. I wished I could go in there every day and try to build my own robot. One shiny white laptop sat in the corner, away from the mess. Dad could have used Robot to help him clean up.

He decided that the Halloween robot would be taller and longer than my robot. It would ride on a base with higher wheels, so it could go over grass. Inside, it would only have a synthesizer and some pulleys to move its dryer-hose arms, so it would be light and easy to lift.

"Good thing I saved this wheel base," Dad said. "It wasn't strong enough to hold the prototype. Here, I'll put on the glue and you hold the body for a few minutes till it sets."

"Mom told me that Robot's a prototype." I was proud of myself for knowing what the word meant. "Something you build to test new ideas. So what's new about it?"

"Mostly vision, which gives it the ability to sort. And a breakthrough in interactivity, of course." Dad was fixing an arm that would trip a synthesizer, so our imitation robot could say "thank you" when candy was put in a basket we would fasten to its wrist. After the glue dried, I cut simple pincher hands out of cardboard and covered them with foil.

"Hand me that nut," Dad said. "It's about the weight of a candy kiss."

He dropped the nut in the basket. A surprisingly sincere "thank you" came through the little speaker Dad had punched into the cardboard body.

"What's interactivity?" I asked.

"Things you teach Robot, like vocabulary, songs, and filling the dishwasher. I designed a new software program to make it capable of learning."

"So why don't you want other people see Robot?" I asked.

"Someone who knows anything about robots would realize your robot is a real innovation. That person might try to steal the program, to make money without doing the work."

I swallowed hard. A small shiver of fear ran through my chest at the thought of Robot being stolen.

Dad opened the shiny white laptop, then tapped a few keys. Strings of symbols and numbers marched up the screen. "See this?" He took my shoulder and steered me toward the screen, looking very proud of himself.

"Christian Fisher would kill his grandmother to get his hands on this program. There's nothing else like it."

We lifted the Halloween robot down from the bench. It looked pretty good, but Dad kept fiddling with it all week long, mostly while I was doing my homework or practicing. Meanwhile the real Robot reminded me to clean out my backpack every day, so Mom and Dad learned about Parents' Night before it happened.

"It's the week after Halloween," Mom told us, holding the orange sheet in her hand. "I'll be in Atlanta, I think, but you should be able to go, Alex."

"You have no idea how much I have to do between now and Thanksgiving!"

"It's all right," I interrupted. "You don't have to go." I actually wished Dad and Mom would go together, but I wanted to keep them from getting into an argument.

"Alex, we haven't been to Parents' Night since Celia was in kindergarten. Most parents go every year. It's a way of supporting the school. Couldn't you spare a few hours for Celia's education?"

Mom made Dad feel guilty enough that he promised to go, and he wrote the date in his computer calendar.

*   *   *

On Halloween night, I put on one of Dad's old lab coats and pulled the fake robot on a cable behind me. Maeve became a portly mama bear in a floppy reddish brown suit. It had a hood with ears that covered her hair and a bear mask that covered her face. Her mama bear was dressed in a big apron and mobcap. She carried her teddy bear on her back in an old baby sling. Jennifer looked the proper princess, with a gauzy dress over her dance leotard, a crown on her smooth brown hair, and glittery high-heeled shoes. We got a lot of candy. The Halloween robot got the most, because people loved hearing it say, "Thank you. Happy Halloween!"

After we'd covered the whole neighborhood, we circled back to Jennifer's house. Dad waited there to drive us home. "Mom will never let me keep all this candy," I told them in the car. "We'll divide it up when we get there."

Up the hill, floodlights were on all around the estate house. Lights washed over a blue van parked in the driveway. Just one window above the carriage house showed a light. Mark Ludlow was home, but I didn't think he and Rocky would welcome trick-or-treaters.

Mom opened the door, dressed in the Halloween costume she'd worn for as long as we could remember: a faded calico dress and embroidered pinafore that once belonged to her great-grandmother from Sweden. Mom held the remote in her hand, and Robot stood beside her, playing a synthesized version of "In the Hall of the Mountain King." Mom had loosely knotted a big orange tie around its neck. We burst into giggles, which made Dad happy.

72

"That Robot has some talent," he said, smiling. He wheeled the imitation robot back to his workshop, where he would take it apart.

When Dad was safely out of earshot, Mom said softly, "Tim came over earlier. He seemed genuinely interested in your robot. Sometime you should give him a good look at it."

I rolled my eyes.

Meanwhile, Maeve curtsied to Mom, staying in character as a polite bear. Her red hair tumbled out when she took off her cap, hood, and mask. Jennifer dropped another curtsy, playing along, but soon pulled off her crown and kicked away her glittery shoes. We dumped the contents of Robot's bag onto the dining room table.

"Dibs on all the kisses!" Jen cried.

"No, I want them," Maeve said, and reached for a handful.

Robot rolled into the dining room, holding a tray of doughnuts. Mom followed, carrying a pitcher of cider in one hand and the remote in the other.

"Let's ask my robot to divvy up," I said.

"I am programmed to sort items," it remarked. "Happy Halloween!"

Jennifer and Maeve, ready to quarrel a second ago, giggled together.

After I'd explained what it should do, Robot delicately held each piece of candy in front of its brown eyes. The blue light flashed. It was slow at first, but whizzed along quickly once it had scanned all the different kinds of candy. It divided each kind equally into three piles while we watched in awe. When it was finished, it said, "Odd pieces are set aside. They may be cut in parts."

We divided up the leftover pieces without an argument.

"This is the best Halloween I've ever had"—Maeve sighed and reached for her fourth doughnut—"thanks to Celia's robot."

9

Robot Goes to School

While Mom played her cello in Atlanta, Dad kept tinkering with Robot and finding more uses for it. He built a vacuum cleaner attachment. "To test its sonar and infrared sensors," he said. Robot did a pretty good job of vacuuming the floors, though we put the glass coffee table out of its way. By now I was in such a routine with Robot that Dad decided he could leave for work very early and let it see me off to school. It learned to French braid both sides of my hair, and because I was getting up early, we had plenty of time. For my breakfast, Dad discovered Morning Munch Energy Bars at the Food Mart. "All the vitamins you need for a day in a single bar," he explained.

I could eat as many Morning Munch bars as I wanted, along with orange juice and cocoa made in the microwave. Dad would take a couple of bars with him to eat in the car on his way to work. Usually he would call me on his cell phone while he was stuck in traffic on Memorial Drive and tell jokes while we were both munching our bars. "It's our way of having breakfast together," he would tell me.

(I always wished I had my own cell phone, but Mom said, "Ask Dad." And Dad always said I was sure to lose it. He was probably right. I did lose a lot of things. But I wished he'd trust me more.)

Robot would see me out the door. I liked hearing, "Good-bye, Celia. Have a lovely day at school," even from a Robot.

Then Robot would close the door behind me and turn on the security system. Our security system was hooked up to the police and fire departments. That wasn't unusual—a lot of houses in our neighborhood did that. But what was unusual was that we never had a false alarm. Dad made sure of that.

Dad kept his promise and took me to Parents' Night at school. Mrs. Flower charged toward us as soon as we entered the classroom. Jen and Maeve were there with their moms and dads. The other kids and their parents stood around the room, admiring displays of our paintings and stories, and looking at Ralph the Iguana in his cage. When Mrs. Flower called, "Mr. Chow, I'm so glad you could come tonight. I've heard how busy you've been," everyone looked up.

Then I was sorry I had ever told Dad about Parents' Night. I wanted to walk out the door, but Dad loved attention. He smiled and shook my teacher's hand.

"Celia is working up to her full potential at last." Mrs. Flower beamed. I guess she noticed that I turned in extra credit math problems every day, and that I was getting more one hundreds on my spelling tests.

"I hear she's getting help from a robot," she went on. I'm not quite sure that Mrs. Flower believed, right then, that Robot actually existed.

"That's right." Dad smiled and nodded, not giving anything away. "It was designed to help with homework."

I knew that Dad was not telling the whole truth. He had designed his prototype for a lot more than helping with homework. He could have programmed my computer to do that. What about sorting and hazardous waste cleanup? What about the things it learned from me? How to navigate the house, all those new words, the songs? What about "the vision thing"? I could never ask those questions while everyone was watching.

Smiling brightly, Mrs. Flower said, "The fifth grade is planning a unit on computers. Of course we want our students to imagine the future of computers, and robots will certainly be part of that future. Would you allow Celia to bring her robot to school?"

I wasn't too worried, because I was sure Dad would tell her it was a valuable prototype and that I couldn't possibly take it outside the house. I'd forgotten about Dad and teachers. Mom says it's because the Chinese respect education more than Americans do. It's connected with something she calls the Confucian work ethic. And Zumu is a teacher. Anyway, he's never liked Mom to criticize my teachers, and he's always telling me I should do what any teacher says.

Dad asked, "What day would be convenient?" Mrs. Flower suggested a day the following week, and before I knew it, I was scheduled to bring Robot into school.

I stood there, not knowing what to think. Partly, I was excited to show off Robot. Partly, I just wanted to sink into the floor. Every kid in school would be staring at Robot, asking me about it, wanting to touch it. No one would leave me alone. Now I wouldn't just be the only Asian kid in my class. I'd be the only kid in the whole school who owned a robot.

Then other parents came up to talk to Mrs. Flower. After Dad had taken a quick look at our classroom, we visited the library, the gym, the art room, and the music room with Jen's parents. Dad always had a good time with Jen's dad, mainly because Mr. Logan always laughed at his jokes. The two dads walked ahead of us, talking about the Red Sox's season as we headed down the main hall on our way out, so Dad didn't see Tim and his mom come out of the sixth-grade corridor.

"Hello, Celia," Mrs. O'Mara said politely. "Is your mom on tour?" I nodded. Mom called Mrs. O'Mara "Black Irish," which means she has black hair and blue eyes. Tim's blond, although he got his eyes from her. Her skin was much whiter than his, as if she never went out in the sun. Standing beside him, she looked small and thin, and really, really tired.

The Calyx van had brought Mom home while I was asleep. She slept late, so I didn't see her until she opened the door for me that afternoon. While I was walking up Heartwright Lane, Rocky rushed down the hill, barking furiously.

"That dog!" Mom closed the door and shook her head. She gave me a hug, a kiss, and a compliment for hanging up my coat and putting away my backpack.

In the kitchen, Mom warmed up a cranberry muffin she'd picked up at the West Haven Bakery, and asked, "Is there a new caretaker up at the Heartwright Estate?"

"You mean that guy with the scruffy ponytail?"

"You've seen him too? Pablo got out today and Rocky went wild. Mark came to haul him up the hill, and this other guy was with him. I was trying to coax Pablo out of the woodpile, so I didn't get a good look at him."

Pablo wound around my ankles, meowing to tell me about his adventure. I picked him up and rubbed my face in his fur. "Stay in the house," I told him. "That dog could kill you."

Dad spent a lot of time in his workshop that weekend, preparing a special demonstration program for Robot, so I got a break from cleaning. "This demo program will be useful when we try to pitch the prototype," he said. He stayed up late the night before Robot's school visit, putting the finishing touches on his software.

The morning Robot went to school, my violin was laid out for Suzuki class, my backpack was neatly organized with all my homework ready, and my coat was lying on top of it. You could still see orange juice stains if you looked hard enough. Mom made her special scrambled eggs and cinnamon toast for breakfast.

"When you want to start the demo, say, 'Robot, please demonstrate your special features,'" Dad told me. He continued with a list of instructions and warnings. I could tell Mom was trying to keep from smiling, or even laughing, because Dad was being so . . . Dad.

"Don't ever try to lift Robot, it's much too heavy," he told me. "Don't let anyone else lift it either. Don't take it on stairs, or grass or mud."

"Good thing it's a sunny day," Mom interrupted. "Snow would make everything harder."

Dad went on as if he hadn't heard her. "Robot will be in a new place. It might run into a child who gets in its way. Be really careful, especially with little ones. Tell them it has a lot of trouble seeing, so it bumps into things. Tell everyone to stay out of its way as you lead it down the hall."

Dad continued his warnings as I got up from the table. He grabbed my arm. "Don't talk about Robot's sorting abilities. Don't tell *anyone* it can tell a block of Lego from a lock."

"Alex," Mom said, "I'm sure Celia will be able to keep Robot safe."

Dad had installed my old car seat into the back of his Volvo. Grunting and muttering, he carefully lifted Robot into the seat and strapped it in. "I hope it won't fall out," he said. "If it falls out, it will be ruined."

It didn't, of course, but when Dad pulled up to the

school, the terriers from the house across the street were loose again. Those terriers are a major pain when they get loose, which is very often. They're so curious and playful that they bug kids who walk to school. They nip your gloves or even your backpack if it's hanging down low enough. To make things even worse, a lady who takes in stray cats lives next door to our school, and the terriers love to chase them. You can't even count the number of cats she has. Her house was there long before Abigail Adams was built, and Jennifer's mom once told me that the police call her whenever they have a cat problem. She has a fence, but the cats will slip through and come to the front of the school, begging for attention.

There weren't any cats in sight that morning, so the dogs rushed up to Dad when he started to open the car door. Dad doesn't like dogs much. He shooed them away, but they thought he was just playing. They jumped and nipped at his hands. He pressed the yellow No Dogs button. I couldn't hear anything, but the smaller terrier put his ears back and slouched between the walkers who filled the sidewalks in front of the school. The bigger one looked at Dad for a long time, then trotted after its companion. Kids waiting for the opening bell stopped to stare at Robot and Dad. The bell rang, but no one went in.

Dad smiled at his audience. He handed me the remote. "Now remember," he said loudly enough for all the kids to hear, "this remote control is only for teachers. Your robot is not a toy!"

"Good-bye, Celia," he said, looking straight into my

eyes. "Take good care of Robot. I'll be right here when you come out."

I wished Robot could make me invisible, but no such luck. Kids crowded around me, asking stupid questions: "Where's its head? How can it go anywhere without legs?"

"It moves on wheels," I answered the third grader who asked that question. I told Robot in a loud, clear voice, "Follow me," and started through the crowd. Kids stepped aside to make way for me and Robot, then followed us into the school's front hall. I never wanted to be a pied piper, but that day I was.

I knew there'd be trouble as soon as I saw Timothy O'Mara coming from the back entrance, where the buses dropped kids off. He had spotted Robot, and was running straight toward us.

10

Robot Meets Tim

"Turn. Increase speed," I prompted Robot, heading for my classroom, praying Robot wouldn't mow down some little first grader before I could escape Tim.

It was impossible. Tim is big for his age, and stocky, so the other kids let him elbow his way through the crowd. A second grader burst into tears. Ignoring her—and me— entirely, he trotted along beside Robot as it wheeled behind me down the corridor.

"Hi, Robot. My name's Tim," he said. "Hear me, Robot? I'm Timothy O'Mara."

"It can't hear you."

"Why not? It heard you."

"It's keyed to my voice," I explained as patiently as I could to someone I wished would go away. "You'd have to sound exactly like me to command it."

All the time, we were moving slowly down the hall. I wasn't looking at Tim. Dad's warnings had rattled me, so I kept turning to watch Robot. I couldn't help hearing

Tim, though, shrilling like a stuck-up sixth-grade girl, "Hey, Robot! Follow me!"

Robot didn't swerve. We were almost to my classroom.

"I saw you give your ugly friend the remote." (He meant Maeve.) "Why not me?" Tim bent down to look Robot in the eye. "Hey, talk to me!" he yelled at it.

Robot kept rolling slowly down the hall.

"Stupid Robot!" Tim kicked Robot hard. Robot didn't stop, but Tim hopped on one foot, holding his sneaker. Mom always said he looked like a choir boy, with his big blue eyes and long lashes. I turned around in fury, and thought I saw tears in his eyes.

By this time we'd created such a stir that teachers were coming out of their classrooms. I heard the principal's voice ring out, telling me to stop the robot.

I did, of course.

"What's going on here?" Mr. Lyman demanded.

I didn't have to say a word. Other kids were eager to tell the story. "Celia was going to her classroom. She didn't do anything. Tim kicked her robot for no reason."

Mr. Lyman looked alarmed. "Timothy," he said sternly. "Our school is fortunate that Mr. Chow allowed Celia to share her robot. I'm told it's quite unique, and there will be serious consequences for anyone who damages it."

"What about me?" Tim protested. "That stupid robot broke my foot!"

"I doubt you've been seriously injured," Mr. Lyman answered. "You can rest your foot by spending recess in my office." He told the kids watching, "Now get along to your classes!"

The late bell rang, and slowly the crowd broke up. I led Robot into my classroom. Just before I went inside, I looked over my shoulder to see Tim walking slowly backward in the direction of the sixth-grade classrooms. His shoulders were slumped; his eyes were fixed on Robot. He looked so sad that I felt just a little bit sorry for him. Maybe he did want to talk to Robot, not just pick on me.

The two other fifth-grade classes came in for Robot's demonstration. It wasn't as hard getting up in front of all those people as I thought it would be. Actually, Mrs. Flower did most of the talking. She had been teaching us about computers and robots, so most of the kids were really interested. All I had to do was answer questions. Once I started talking about Robot, I forgot that everyone was looking at me.

First I explained about the camcorder eye and the radar and sonar sensors it used to figure out where it was going. I remembered not to say anything about Legos and locks. Instead I told the class, "It has a lot of trouble seeing and it sometimes bumps into things."

Then I used the remote to make it pace up and down the rows. As it passed each desk, kids stared and patted it shyly. When it got to the back of the class, I put down the remote and called out, "Robot, come back to the front of the class. Move forward beside the windows."

As it rolled along, I explained, "It can only understand one voice. Even though my dad designed it, it doesn't hear his voice."

"How does he communicate with it?" Mrs. Flower asked. She watched nervously as Robot rolled dangerously close to Ralph the Iguana's glass cage. Every head in the classroom was turned toward Robot.

"Robot," I called out, "avoid all objects."

"Complying," it answered, and swerved into open space. Kids laughed, and Mrs. Flower looked relieved.

I answered Mrs. Flower so that the class could hear. "My dad uses a special laptop for programming."

Robot stopped beside me in front of the class. "Robot," I said, "please demonstrate your special features."

It swiveled around to face everyone and said in its bouncy synthesized voice: "Good morning, boys and girls. I am happy to be here to show you what a robot does. I hope you will enjoy my visit to your classroom."

Everyone laughed. Dad's demo program kicked in.

Robot started a stiff kind of dance, swiveling its brown camcorder eyes. Using its pincher hands to point at its body, it chanted in its perkiest voice, bouncing to the rhythm of its words: "This is my sound receiver, this is my keyboard, this is a smoke detector, this repels dogs, this sharpens pencils, this finds buried metal."

Cries of "oh wow!" or "cool!" came from all over the classroom.

Roger Ennis said, "Let's look for gold at recess." Only Roger would think of that. Roger's not bad, for a boy.

When Robot stopped bouncing and chanting, I said to it, "Please give us a weather report."

"Today is sunny, with a high of forty-one degrees Fahrenheit. Tomorrow there will be a chance of snow, with a high of thirty-nine degrees Fahrenheit." I noticed that it was speaking with more expression than when I first got it.

"Can it carry heavy things for you?" Mrs. Flower asked.

"No, it can't lift anything heavy," I told her. To prove it, I put my backpack on the floor and asked it to lift the object in front of it. It reached down and tried.

"Attempting to lift this object would cause damage." It sounded almost apologetic. More laughter from the class.

"It can't lift heavy objects, but it can dust the ceiling lights," I told Mrs. Flower. I'd heard her complain that the custodians never did that.

She pulled a dust cloth from her desk. "Show us," she said.

I spread the cloth over its right hand and ordered, "Wipe the ceiling."

The extension shot up. Its wrist flexed. Astonished noises came from the classroom. Robot carefully but thoroughly wiped the fluorescent lights hanging from the high classroom ceiling.

Then it was time for recess. As the other fifth graders went back to their classrooms to get their coats, Maeve, Jennifer, and Roger waited for me and Robot so that we could try the metal detector. I was putting on my coat when Mrs. Ketchum, the school secretary, came into the room.

"Mr. Lyman wants to see you and your robot right now," she told me.

I felt like someone was squeezing my throat. Was I going to get in trouble for what happened earlier? Everyone else went out for recess, while Robot and I followed Mrs. Ketchum down the hall.

It turned out Mr. Lyman was making Tim apologize. That was so embarrassing.

"Sorry I kicked the robot Mr. Chow made," Tim mumbled reluctantly, staring at the floor. All the time I was wondering what he'd do to me on the bus the next morning.

I muttered, "It's okay," and was ready for a fast exit, but Mr. Lyman had other ideas. It sounded like he wanted to start a heart-to-heart talk, which made me even more nervous.

"Timothy doesn't express himself very well," Mr. Lyman said, while Tim rolled his eyes behind the principal's back. "But he is actually very interested in your robot. Could you give him an opportunity to manipulate it?" Over Mr. Lyman's shoulder, Tim glared at me.

I opened my mouth to say that I'd promised Dad I wouldn't let any other kid touch Robot. But Dad didn't ride the bus with Tim, and the principal was asking.

"Sure," I answered. "Dad fixed up this remote control." I handed it to Mr. Lyman, sort of keeping my promise to Dad. He handed the remote to Tim.

"It's set on low speed," I told Mr. Lyman. "You press the arrows to make it move forward, backward, left, and right. The red button makes it stop."

"Try it, Tim," Mr. Lyman said.

Tim did. He moved Robot forward, brought it to a stop, and moved it back. He didn't say anything, but he looked like he'd forgotten there was anything else around him but Robot. Robot turned its camcorder eyes in his direction, trying to "see" who was directing it. I felt just a little bit jealous.

"How do you get it to talk?" he asked Mr. Lyman.

Mr. Lyman gave me a significant look. Much as I hated to, I said, "Robot, this is Timothy."

"How do you do, Timothy," Robot replied.

Tim's eyes widened, and he stopped looking so angry.

"Uh, hi, Robot," Tim replied.

I've never been so happy to hear the bell that ends recess. I held out my hand for the remote, and Tim passed it over. "Celia, would you let me—" he began. Before he could go any farther, I turned away and hurried Robot out of the principal's office to my classroom.

11

Robot to the Rescue

Mrs. Flower always taught math after recess. The other fifth grades stayed in their own classrooms, so we had Robot all to ourselves. It moved from desk to desk, offering its keyboard to each kid. Everyone was very careful and serious. I think the kids had a hard time remembering that Robot was a machine and not a person.

Robot went with us to art, where Mr. Montgomery told us to draw Robot in two different poses: saluting the flag, and stretching its extension arm to full length. Then he asked us to draw or paint an imaginary picture of what we would like Robot to do. Roger showed Robot finding lots of gold coins and making him rich. Maeve showed Robot flying over the town with her on its back. Jen imagined Robot as a cook, making her favorite meal. I sketched a picture of me with Dad's laptop, programming Robot to be less bossy.

Robot stayed in our classroom while we went to lunch. I worried about leaving it in an unlocked room, and then I worried about taking it out to recess where all the kids could see it. But I had promised Jen, Maeve, and Roger. The fifth and sixth grade had lunch recess together, so as soon as we rolled Robot out on the asphalt section, I looked around for Tim. There's a softball field in a park next to our school. Tim was playing stickball out there with a bunch of sixth-grade boys, so he was too far away to bother me.

Robot extended its metal detector and found five dimes and four quarters, a silver dollar, and a man's gold ring in the school yard dirt. Mrs. Flower gave the ring and the silver dollar to Mrs. Ketchum. I gave up trying to keep the remote to myself. Eventually, almost every fifth grader had a chance to use the remote control to move Robot around, no matter what Dad said. I watched Robot zip around the asphalt section of the playground, thinking, Too bad Dad will never know how well it gets around outdoors.

After lunch recess, our class had a music lesson. A few of us, including Maeve and me, didn't go to the music room with the others. Instead, we took our violins to a small room where Mrs. Eastman was waiting for the Suzuki kids. We started by bowing to her, as we always did. Robot could not bend, so I had taught it to put its hands together, do a little forward and back roll, and say, "Good afternoon, Mrs. Eastman."

Mrs. Eastman bowed back. "Welcome to Suzuki class," she said, smiling a little doubtfully. She got all excited when I told her about Robot's metronome, though. She told me what tempo to set, and we all played "Lightly Row" together.

Back in our classroom, Mrs. Flower asked everyone

to contribute to a class description of Robot. She wrote everyone's comments on a big chart. My day at school with Robot was almost over.

We always sang songs in the last fifteen minutes of class. I told Mrs. Flower that I had taught Robot some of my favorites: "You Are My Sunshine" and "Michael, Row the Boat Ashore." The class sang those songs along with Robot. When the bell rang, everyone was in a good mood.

So it would have been a perfect day if only Dad had been there when Robot and I came out of school.

Dad usually arrives at places early, but this time he was late. Stuck in traffic, I found out later, caused by an accident on Route 2. When I didn't see his car, I shrugged off my backpack and dumped it next to the wall, along with my violin. Maeve, Robot, and I waited just outside the front entrance as students poured out. Jen, a walker, stayed to keep us company. As they passed out of the building, some kids touched Robot or stopped to ask about it.

We watched a cute kindergarten girl on the lawn in front of the school pick up a small black cat with white paws. Her friends stood around her, waiting for a turn to pet it. It must have come from the cat lady's house, because it was always hanging around after school so that kids would pay attention to it. The cat lady had so many cats that she probably didn't have time to cuddle them all.

I was thinking what it must be like to have so many cats inside one house when Jen whispered in my ear:

"Looks like Tim skipped the bus." I glanced sideways to see Tim lurking at the edge of the crowd, staring at Robot. I felt a small shiver of fear. Then Maeve distracted me.

"We're in for a thrilling afternoon of neighborhood beautification." Maeve could always roll out the big words. She nodded at the third-grade Scouts gathered near their leaders, who were handing out plastic bags with a recycling logo.

"They'll have their picture in the paper tomorrow," Jennifer said as a blond woman holding a camera started arranging the Scouts.

I pulled Maeve and Jen beside me in front of Robot. I didn't want the photographer to find another interesting subject for pictures. Across the street, the terriers were barking and pushing at their gate. I realized they'd been doing that ever since we came out. Were they after Robot or the kitten? I got all trembly wondering.

Suddenly, the gate swung open, and the terriers lunged across the street, rushing toward the kindergartners and the little cat. The girl holding the cat tried to protect it, but it jumped from her arms. From the sound of her screams, it must have given her a nasty scratch.

It all happened so fast. The cat—it was hardly more than a kitten—streaked toward the little tree growing in front of the school. The terriers followed, barking like crazy. The cat tried to climb the tree, but it couldn't get a good hold, and I thought the terriers were going to get it. I pressed Robot's No Dogs button.

Both terriers stopped for an instant, whining. The noise must have startled the young cat, too, because she lost her grip and slid down the tree. The small dog ran off right away, but the bigger one hesitated for a moment, then put both front paws on the tree trunk, barking savagely as the little cat slid helplessly down, trying to hang on but failing.

Moving faster than I could think, I raised Robot's base and shouted, "Robot, grab the cat *now!*"

Robot whizzed toward the tree, extended one arm above the growling dog, grabbed the cat by the loose skin on its back, just like it did our toys, and raised it high in the air. The big dog barked and jumped, but it couldn't reach the cat, which twisted and snarled and tried to bite Robot. I hoped the poor thing wouldn't die of fright!

By this time everyone was watching. The Scouts forgot about posing for their cleanup picture and ran to see what was going on. Tim stayed beside the school. Other kids cheered, the crossing guard clapped, and the photographer rushed over to snap a picture.

One of the Scout leaders grabbed the big dog firmly by its collar and led it home. She looked like someone who was used to handling dogs. The cat lady, a small woman in sneakers and sweatshirt and pants covered with cat hair, banged out her front door, wide-eyed and panting. She ran to her picket fence as I led Robot, holding the limp cat, over to her. The cat's eyes were glazed with fright, but it was panting, so I knew it was alive.

"Release the cat," I told Robot, who put the kitten gently into her waiting hands.

Meanwhile, the photographer was asking, "Who's that girl with the robot?" when Dad drove up.

He didn't bother to ask what was going on. He took one look at the camera, grabbed the remote control, and rushed Robot toward the car. The photographer tried to ask my name and his name, but he shouted, "No comment, nothing to say!"

Dad's face turned red. A vein throbbed in his forehead.

"Dad, the dogs would have killed—"

"Did she take a picture?" Dad yelled, chopping up the words like he was speaking Chinese.

"I think so."

"What newspaper she from?"

"I don't know," I answered, almost in tears.

"This is outrageous!" Dad shouted, as he strained to lift Robot into the car. Maeve crept around the car and slipped quietly into the backseat.

As I got in on the curb side, I heard the Scout leaders say, "Come on boys, get busy." Walkers started heading home. I didn't turn around to look for Tim.

As we drove away, there was no point in explaining about the Scouts and neighborhood beautification. Dad was much too angry to listen. Maeve and I sat silently in the backseat, with Robot between us, while Dad ranted. "That was a gross invasion of privacy! These photographers just take pictures of everything they see!" I looked down at my lap, wishing I could fold up and disappear. I was so ashamed.

By the time we dropped Maeve off, Dad's outburst had turned to angry silence. He parked in front of her house and sat, gripping the steering wheel and staring straight ahead while she got out and I whispered good-bye. As soon as she closed the car door, he didn't wait for her to go into her house. He gunned the engine and drove to Heartwright Lane without saying a single word.

12

My Closet, At Last

"How could she understand, if you've never really explained about vision? Or that interactivity you're so proud of?" Mom yelled back, lingering on each syllable of that long word.

Dad had been shouting in the kitchen a long time before Mom could interrupt him. Her voice sounded clear and sharp over the rush of running water. She'd been putting a chicken in the oven when we came into the house, and now she was cleaning up. Robot and I had quickly retreated to my room.

Pablo came out from where he had been sleeping under my bed and started to purr. I sat down and stroked him, feeling guilty and scared. I thought about the little cat dangling from Robot's arm extension. Had it been injured? With Dad so upset, I felt like I had made a complete mess of everything, even rescuing the cat. I was ashamed of myself. And I was angry at Dad because he blamed me for something that really wasn't my fault. I wanted to pretend the whole thing had never happened. I wanted to do something ordinary, normal, like homework.

My homework was in my backpack. But where was my backpack? And my violin?

I looked around my room, but I knew I hadn't brought it in the house. Had I left it in the car? I couldn't remember. I had to go and check.

"Don't you ever listen to me? I just told you she's too young to understand!" Dad paced through the kitchen, into the dining room, and back. He was still red in the face. I stopped in the vestibule, but Mom and Dad didn't seem to see me.

"Alex, you're making way too much of this." Mom looked straight at Dad, exasperated. "I don't think she's too young to understand that you don't want the world to know you've made an interactive robot that can tell a cat from a dog!"

Dad stopped pacing and stared at Mom, then looked at me, and back at Mom again. His face relaxed. He almost smiled.

I'd been afraid to say anything up to that moment. Every word I'd been holding back tumbled out. "It wasn't my idea to take Robot to school," I yelled, fighting back tears. "And it wasn't my fault that the photographer was there. I didn't know she'd come. When I saw her, I stood in front of Robot. But when the dogs came after the cat, I didn't want her to be killed like the Levins' barn cats."

I couldn't stop myself. I started to cry. "And now I've lost my violin and my backpack!" I sobbed even harder.

Mom took me in her arms. She hugged and kissed me, sat me down on a stool beside the counter, and put a tissue box in front of me.

The sound of our doorbell ringing startled us all. Dad reached it in two steps and flung it open, then stood there, staring down. I craned my head around to see who was at the door.

No one. Just my backpack and violin, sitting on the front walk. And a boy running down Heartwright Lane. Tim.

All in one moment I remembered. I'd left my backpack in front of the school. Tim had certainly missed our bus while he watched Robot rescue the kitten, so he must have walked all the way home carrying my backpack and violin.

Dad hefted my backpack. "What are these doing here?" he asked.

"I took off my backpack while I was waiting for you. When you got mad in front of Maeve and all the kids, I was so embarrassed, I forgot everything else. Tim O'Mara just brought it back." I started to cry again. I hated the thought of Tim handling my backpack. Had he looked inside? Yet he'd carried it all the way to my front door.

"That was very kind of Tim," Mom said. "You should be sure to thank him tomorrow."

Dad had already stopped thinking about Tim. He settled on a stool beside me and put his arm around my shoulders. "Celia, I'm sorry I yelled at you. I was so frustrated, getting stuck in traffic, and when I saw that photographer . . ." Dad didn't finish his sentence.

"Want a cup of tea?" Mom asked him as she put the kettle on.

"It's never been done before," Dad said.

"What?" I asked. I had stopped crying, but my voice still quavered.

"No one's ever been able to make a robot that could tell a cat from a dog. Moria Systems has no competition now. Zero. Zilch."

The kettle whistled. Mom put a pinch of Chinese tea in the bottom of a mug and poured water over it. She set the cup gently in front of Dad, and he took a sip. He spoke directly to me. "Moria Systems is bidding on a very profitable international contract for high-tech recycling. We need a robot that can make discriminations, so it can sort through old landfills for anything worth reclaiming."

He swirled the tea around in his cup to cool it. "Remember what I've always said? If a job is dangerous, dirty, or dull, build a robot to do it. But first we have to figure out how to mass-produce some version of Robot. I've just made a significant improvement on vision and sorting capacity. It's hard to measure interactivity, which is the wave of the future in robotics. Your robot is riding high, though. I'm amazed how much it's taught you and how much it's learned from you. You showed it how to tell a cat from a dog."

I blew my nose and used a fresh tissue to wipe the tears off my cheeks. When I heard Dad praising me, I felt a whole lot better.

"It baby-sits and vacuums too. And does French braids." Mom smiled.

Now Dad sounded much calmer. "I should never have let my prototype out of the house. From now on, I won't, no matter who asks."

"I don't think the photographer would use the picture if she couldn't get permission from the subject," Mom said. "I'm guessing she works for *The Villager*. You know, that free newspaper I get sometimes at Nature's Bounty? Not the place your average industrial thief would pick up secrets."

"Anyway, the robot's safe inside the house now," Dad said. "And its program is on my laptop, which is locked in my workshop."

He sipped his tea and stared off into space. The smile that had started earlier returned. "A robot that can tell a cat from a dog," he said. "They said it couldn't be done."

Mom poured herself a glass of wine and lifted it to Dad, toasting him and smiling. "And you've done it," she said.

I'm the one who showed Robot how, I thought, but I didn't say it out loud. Still, I didn't feel so guilty anymore.

The next morning, as Tim thumped down the school bus aisle, I forced myself to look up at him. "Uh, thanks for picking up my backpack and violin."

He swung into the seat behind me. "You left them at school," he said. "Your backpack sure is heavy. What do you keep in there, bricks?"

"I bring home stuff I need to do homework," I said, looking out the window to see Maeve waiting at her stop. Tim was so irritating. He couldn't just do me a favor, he had to complain about it.

"Does Robot help?" he asked as Maeve took her seat beside me.

I took her arm and whispered in her ear, "Ignore him."

"I bet your robot couldn't do sixth-grade homework." I knew Tim was trying to get my goat. I pretended I didn't hear him.

"I bet he does your homework for you," Tim yelled over the seat. "You're so ditzy, you can't even remember your backpack."

All the way to school, Maeve and I whispered non-sense in each other's ears deliberately, just to annoy him. At least we got him to keep quiet. I could see him out of the corner of my eye looking out the bus window with his mouth all tight. If he'd been anyone but Tim, I might have thought he looked sad.

The first thing Friday morning, Mrs. Flower pinned a clipping from *The Villager* on the bulletin board. There it was: a picture of Robot holding the cat. I stood beside it, the only Asian kid in the picture, looking really dumb. The headline read, ROBOT RESCUES CAT. The story under the headline wasn't long: "A robot belonging to an unidentified student at Abigail

Adams Elementary School rescued a cat from a pair of playful dogs yesterday. The owner of the robot declined to be interviewed, but the owner of the cat, Mrs. Florence Treat, said gratefully, 'The robot saved my little Bootsie's life.'"

I couldn't swallow. I felt cold and trembly. Now Dad would really have something to be angry about.

I decided I wouldn't tell him, and I hoped he wouldn't find the story on his own. Calyx had a weekend engagement in Providence, so Mom wouldn't be grocery shopping. Dad might rush over to the Food Mart over in East Haven, but they never put out *The Villager.* Even if they did, Dad might not notice it. He lived in his own world most of the time. I told myself that Mom had to be right. No one into robotics would ever read *The Villager,* would they? Still, every time I thought of that picture, I felt a cold shiver of worry. I kept it to myself, and it wouldn't go away.

It didn't help that when we were going home, Tim yelled so the whole bus could hear, "Snobby Celia has a famous robot!" Where had Tim seen that picture? Were all the teachers showing it to their students? I looked out the window, trying to ignore him. Maeve patted my arm to comfort me.

When we got off the bus, I was glad to see Tim run straight to his house. I walked up Heartwright Lane under dark gray clouds that sent down needles of icy rain. I kept my head down until I heard Rocky barking. The sound didn't come from up the hill, but from close to my house. I looked up and started with fear.

The scruffy guy in the blue knit cap pushed his way

out of the bushes beside Dad's workshop, holding Rocky by the collar. I recognized the greasy ponytail falling out of his cap. The collar of his worn jacket was turned up, and his cap was pulled down, so I could hardly see his face. Rocky lunged toward me, straining against his collar and barking.

"Hey." Scruffy Guy greeted me without expression. "Dog got loose. Chased him down here."

I stood still, shaking inside. If I moved closer to the house, Robot would open the door, and I didn't want this guy to see it. "Keep that dog away from our house," I said. I felt scared, but also angry. "He's a cat-killer."

He grunted and dragged Rocky along Heartwright Lane. He was pretty rough, though I can't say I felt too sorry for Rocky. When they'd turned onto Woodland Road, and were out of sight, I ran to the front door. Robot opened it. I rushed inside and closed it quickly behind me.

Mom came out of the guest room to give me a hug.

"That scruffy guy and Rocky were lurking around our house," I told her. "He said Rocky got loose, but it seemed kind of weird."

Mom frowned. "Well, I suppose he's telling the truth. Rocky's certainly gotten out before. But I don't like strangers hanging around our house." She sighed. "Still, it's probably better not to mention it to Dad. He's already so wound up. I'm afraid he might call Mrs. Prentice in Florida and get her in a snit."

I didn't want to see Dad get mad, like he did the day

I took Robot to school. It really was easier not to tell him things that would upset him.

At dinner, Mom made a long speech about how lucky I was to have so much stuff. "There are a lot of children in East Haven, and even some in West Haven, who get all their Christmas presents at the PTA sale." She said this every year.

"The sale is a week from tomorrow." Mom shook her head. "Where has the year gone?"

"Won't you be in New York that day?" Dad asked. "You're certainly one busy woman." He didn't sound like he was giving her a compliment.

I had almost forgotten. Some really rich guy in New York City had offered Calyx a huge fee if they would play at his Thanksgiving weekend open house. Mom said he wanted to impress his new girlfriend. I would be staying with Zumu the whole weekend.

Mom ignored Dad. "I'd like to deliver our donations on Monday or Tuesday. Celia, I want you and Robot to clean out your closet. Starting tomorrow morning."

"Since I have to stay home anyway, I'll be able to assess Robot's capacities," Dad said, and this time he seemed to be complimenting himself.

Saturday turned out to be dark, cold, and so rainy that I worried about Mom riding to Providence in the Calyx van. It was a perfect day to start digging into my closet. I hadn't seen the bottom since I started first grade.

Robot had a plan. It told me to get some rubber

bands, a broom, and a dust pan. I didn't know what it needed rubber bands for. "Hang extraneous hangers over my arm," it ordered, shooting out its extension arm horizontally. I had no idea how many hangers were mixed up with the stuff in my closet! I thought I was finished, but Robot peered into my closet with its camcorder eyes and blinking blue light and told me to check again. Would you believe I found seven more?

"Set aside ten hangers and use the rubber bands to tie the rest in bundles." With all those hangers out of the way, it was easier to get into my closet. Robot reached in and picked up random articles of clothing and asked me the same questions for each one. "Do you plan to wear this again? Is it clean?" It told me to hang up clean clothes on hangers, not drape them over my closet rod. Dirty clothes went in the laundry basket. When it found clothes I'd outgrown, like a pair of Oshkosh overalls I hadn't worn since third grade, I dumped them into a shopping bag.

Clothes filled up three shopping bags. Once we got rid of every hanger, Robot extended its arm and rummaged around in the closet, pulling things out. A loom that had fallen on Dad's head last September went into a shopping bag. Two creepy-eyed blond dolls Aunt Gail once sent me followed. My dear old Raggedy Ann doll went to sit on my bed. I couldn't bear to give her away.

After a while, we got down to the closet floor. Robot pulled out every shoe it found there. I matched them up, then filled another shopping bag with the shoes I'd out-grown. Finally I could get a broom inside to sweep the floor. I found bits of the locks I'd taken apart, lost game parts, more Lego blocks, and pieces of old puzzles. I even found the train Dad gave me when I turned seven. And, scrunched up in the back corner, a Red Sox baseball cap—the one Tim had given me at my fourth birthday party. I slammed it down on top of the shoes. Yuck!

Good thing the floor of my room wasn't covered with junk anymore, because we needed the whole area to orga-nize everything. Robot passed each little item in front of its camcorder eyes and blinking blue light, then sorted them into piles. I threw lots and lots of things away. By the time Dad came out of his workshop to see how we were doing, Robot was vacuuming my oriental carpet.

I flung out my arm, proudly pointing to my closet. Even I had forgotten how deep it was. I had stored my easel in the back until next summer, stacked my picture books and art supplies on the top shelf, along with some games I wanted to keep, and hung my clothes neatly in the front of my closet, blouses together, jeans together, dresses together. I had paired up my shoes on their shoe rack. One clean nightgown hung on a hook.

"Wow!" said Dad. After admiring my closet for a minute, he turned to survey all the stuff Robot had been sorting. "So you found the locks I took off our doors when I put in the security system. I'd forgotten all about them."

Then Mr. Weissman called. While he and Dad

talked, Robot and I finished vacuuming. I gave Robot a big hug and yelled, "We did it!"

"Project successful." Robot actually lifted up its dryer-hose arms to gently hug me back while it played a few bars of "Ode to Joy."

I really did feel better after cleaning out my closet. Lighter, freer, with more space around me somehow—like stepping out of a muddy hole to a wide-open lawn. And proud of myself, instead of always feeling helpless, in a mess. Robot had held things up and asked questions, but I had made my own decisions.

Mom got back from Providence Sunday night. She was really excited about my closet. She delivered all the shopping bags to school, along with ten puzzle boxes, my old MindMate computer, and the radio I'd put together. The box of Lego blocks went too, though I wouldn't have been surprised to find more pieces multiplying under the carpet.

We always spent Thanksgiving in Brookline with Zumu, even when Grandmary and Grandpop were home. Zumu reserved the private dining room at Four Seas, her favorite Chinese restaurant. No one ever looked at a menu, because Zumu had already decided what we would eat. I knew she'd order a dish of my favorite Chinese greens. There would be Peking duck, and Dad would say he could make it better. I wouldn't know, because he's never cooked it for me. Also prawns; and chicken with those big, dark Chinese mushrooms; sizzling rice soup; and a whole fish with ginger and other spices. Everyone would pick off pieces with their chopsticks, and there would be great drama when someone turned over the fish.

Mom and Dad drove back to West Haven that night and left me with Zumu. On Friday, Zumu and I took the T to Cambridge, so I could buy Christmas presents with the money Dad gave me. On Saturday I woke up early to join Zumu for her morning tai chi exercises. "Tai chi makes me calm," she told me over the soupy rice porridge she always made. "When I was your age I was too active. I rushed into things without thinking. Got into trouble too." She smiled, remembering her life in Shanghai.

Dad called from the lab twice a day to see how I was doing. I told him I was having a great time, but I missed Maeve and Jen. When I got home on Sunday, I called Jen to tell her about the new clothes Zumu bought me to put in my cleaned-out closet. She told me about the PTA sale. "Did you see anyone buying my computer?" I asked her.

"It was already sold when we got there," she told me. Who bought it? I wondered.

The Calyx van delivered Mom later that evening. Dad picked up a dinner she had ordered from a take-out place on Church Street: turkey, mashed potatoes and gravy, green beans with almonds, and pecan pie. So we had another Thanksgiving dinner, cozy and together at home. If I'd had to choose between my two Thanksgivings, Chinese and American, I couldn't say which one I liked better.

After Thanksgiving, the weather turned colder, and Robot started to remind me to put on my heavy jacket and snow boots. But there wasn't any snow, just rain that sometimes turned to ice. Nothing worth canceling school over. I didn't mind school so much, but I did hate riding the school bus. Every day, Tim sat behind me and bugged me about Robot. He asked so many questions. "Hey, Celia, why did your Dad freak out when he picked you up?" And, "What can your robot see? Can it see faces? Can it tell a boy from a girl?" Usually I ignored him or whispered with Maeve.

Almost every day now, Tim walked directly from our bus stop up the hill to the Heartwright Estate, where Scruffy Guy waited for him at the barn. One morning, when Maeve was home sick, I asked Tim a question: "Who's the guy I always see up at the barn? The one with the blue cap and ponytail."

He leaned forward and rested his arms on the back of my seat. "Name's Jude. Mark hired him to help for the winter." Unfortunately, when I spoke to him I only encouraged him to ask the question I'd been dreading: "Hey, Celia, why won't you let me *work* with your robot?"

I turned my head sideways, not looking at him. At least he'd remembered Robot was not a toy to play with. "Dad doesn't want anyone else to see it," I whispered angrily.

"You took it to school. You showed it to your class. All the fifth graders made it move. Why not me? I'm a boy. I bet you don't know as much about computers as I do. Your snobby scientist dad should know that boys are better with robots than dumb, ditzy girls."

I looked out my window. My throat choked up. I

didn't want to cry. Dad hadn't taught me much about programming. Maybe that was why. Maybe Dad thought that programming was too hard for a girl.

"Just you wait. Someday I'll have a robot to boss around. And I'll never let you touch it."

I wished Tim would disappear from this planet, or even better, the entire universe.

13

Christmas with Robot

Christmas is Mom's favorite holiday. She says a midwinter celebration is in her genes. All her ancestors came from Sweden and Scotland, where they celebrated the solstice to break up the long, dark winter. But sometimes she gets carried away with preparations, which make her tired and cranky. Not this year, with Robot around.

Robot helped when Maeve and Jennifer came over to my house to make Christmas cookies. They've done that ever since we were all in kindergarten, and we always get frosting all over the kitchen. That usually bothers Mom, but Robot went to work with a big sponge attached to its arm extension, and she laughed instead of looking all tight and tense.

After Mom and I brought our Christmas tree home, Robot helped again. Dad fixed it on the stand while Robot and I held it steady. I didn't hear Dad complain once about what a crooked tree we bought, or that we shouldn't be cutting down a tree to celebrate a holiday. Robot used its extension arm to help hang Mom's fragile antique ornaments up high, out of Pablo's reach. Once we showed it how, Robot gripped each one delicately in its left-hand pinchers, felt the tree branch with its fingers, and looped the hook over the branch. Dad and Pablo watched from a distance.

Dad never helps us trim the tree. To quote Mom, "It just isn't his thing." But Robot did help us, so I guess Dad should get some credit. When we finished, Dad said, "Now that is one smart robot I've designed!"

"And Celia and I decorated a beautiful tree," Mom said, stretching her arms above her head, then pulling me into a sideways hug. "It feels so good to have time for everything." Mom would be home for two whole weeks after vacation, getting ready for her solo recital at MIT.

"Be careful, you might get used to it," Dad said.

"Could we teach Robot another Christmas carol now?" I asked, not very sure she'd say yes. I knew she was worried about her recital, and we had been so busy with the tree that she hadn't played her cello that day.

"Sure." She smiled. "But first let's play one ourselves, as a duet." She leafed through her book of Christmas music. Mom never played songs like "Rudolph, the Red-Nosed Reindeer."

"How about 'Silent Night'?" Mom asked.

"Too slow. I like 'Deck the Halls' better. It's got more pep," Dad said.

"We'll play them both." Mom laid out the music for

"Silent Night" on the piano, then moved her cello close to the bench where I sat. Mom is very hard on herself when she plays, but she's usually pretty easy on me. Not like Mrs. Eastman, who yells at the school orchestra when kids goof off. Mom just stops when we get off track and goes back to the beginning. While we stopped and started, Dad went to his workshop to make some phone calls. After we'd played both carols straight through, I taught Robot the words to "Deck the Halls." Dad came to listen, applaud, and sing along: "'Tis the season to be *jia li*." It's an old joke, one he makes every Christmas. *Jolly* sounds like the Chinese words that mean "stay at home."

The last day before Christmas vacation, on the bus home, Tim bugged me with questions. "Did your dad make Robot at home? Will he ever make another one?" I answered with words Mom suggested: "My dad doesn't want me to talk about Robot."

"What's the big secret?" Tim asked. I ignored him, but he kept it up. He boasted, like he had all week, "I'll have a robot of my own pretty soon. Better than yours!"

Where would Tim ever get a robot? I knew Mrs. O'Mara didn't have any extra money to spend.

When the bus stopped, Tim jumped up to be first off, pushing past kids in front of him. By the time I got out, he'd already started up the hill toward the mansion, to help Jude, I guess.

I wondered if he liked the guy. Mom said Tim hung around with Mark because he was looking for a substitute dad. I wondered if he felt the same way about Jude. Personally, I thought both of them were lame substitutes for Tim's real dad, who got a medal for bravery after he died.

I skipped up to our front door. When Robot saw me it started singing in its a bouncy, synthesized voice, "Deck the halls with boughs of holly . . ." Mom and Dad stood close together in the vestibule. Dad had his arm around Mom's waist as he joined in, "'Tis the season to be *jia li.*" At that moment, I felt purely and completely happy.

Neither Maeve nor Jen thought the pun was as funny as we did when I told them about it, but then our Christmas is different from theirs. For starters, I stay up half the night on Christmas Eve at Zumu's apartment with her friends and their kids playing this Chinese gambling game with ivory dominoes. The grown-ups bet dollars and the kids bet small change. If a grown-up wins big, a kid usually gets the money, because they're all friends and no one wants to beat out friends. Mom doesn't go anymore. She doesn't gamble and she doesn't speak Chinese.

She told Dad and me to go to Zumu's and have fun. She'd be much happier staying home to practice for the recital. "After I've played enough Bach, Robot can help me set the table for Christmas dinner tomorrow. Be sure to leave me the remote," she said. "I'll be at Zumu's next week anyway. Christmas is my holiday, New Year's is Dad's." It didn't matter that the real Chinese New Year wouldn't come for a month. Zumu celebrated December 31 just like Chinese New Year.

The bad thing about that Christmas with Robot was that Grandmary and Grandpop were so far away. We had never celebrated Christmas without them. I think Mom would have been less nervous about her recital if Grandmary and Grandpop had been around to cheer her up.

After staying up late on Christmas Eve, I slept in on Christmas morning, but I woke with a start, jumped out of bed, threw on my robe, and ran down to the kitchen. "Where's Robot?" I asked Mom, who was stirring together rice and mushrooms for Christmas dinner.

"With Dad, in his workshop." Mom smiled mysteriously. "It's part of your Christmas present. He said to tell him when you finish breakfast." I rolled my eyes. Dad could stay in his workshop all day, even on Christmas, if we let him.

The best thing Robot did that Christmas was deliver presents. Mom made a wreath of holly big enough to rest over its dome.

After we settled down in the living room to open our gifts, I bent down and whispered in Robot's microphone, "Play your music."

While Robot piped "Santa Claus Is Coming to Town," I chose a package from under the tree for Robot to carry. It rolled over to Mom, stopped playing music, and spoke: "This is a present for Mother."

"Why, thank you," Mom answered, laughing as she took a bright red box from its hands.

"Did anyone notice that it can tell us apart?" Dad asked. "It's a robot like no other!"

Robot went back and forth across the living room, playing the Santa Claus song quietly, but with a jaunty tempo, until we each had a stack of gifts. Even Pablo had little packages from Jennifer and Grandmary. I got lots of great presents. Mom and Dad gave me a sun-and-moon watch and a whole bunch of new art supplies to replace the ones I'd used up and finally thrown away. Grandmary had sent good books, including another Little House book, *These Happy Golden Years*. Dad laughed when I unwrapped Grandmary's present to Pablo: a small toy robot. Jen gave him three new toy mice. He loves to chase them, because they look like the real thing, but he's always losing them under the carpets.

The best present I got came from Dad, a heavy box with an envelope stuck under the ribbon. It was too heavy for Robot to lift, so I left it under the tree. Mom must have wrapped it, because Dad never wraps presents. "Robot has part of the gift in its memory," Dad told me. Mystified, I unwrapped the heavy box and found it filled with brass pin tumblers, knobs, cylinders, and keys.

I must have looked puzzled, because Dad got up and crouched beside me to explain. "I visited Hal, the locksmith at MIT. I used to hang out in his shop a lot. I told him how you liked to take locks apart, and he gave me these old models. Some of them are pretty complicated. Now open the envelope," he added, looking almost mischievous.

Inside was a small, narrow leather wallet, holding things I'd only dreamed of owning: a set of torsion wrenches and picks. Dad watched closely as I drew them out. "Hal told me where to order these only after I swore to him I'd make you promise never to use them illegally." I stared at Dad, speechless with delight.

Dad stood up. "Hal put me on to the best websites for locksmiths, and I transferred the essentials into Robot's memory this morning. It can help you if you get stuck."

Later, Mom called Grandmary and Grandpop, and I listened on the kitchen phone. "Only Celia would be excited about locks and keys." Grandpop chuckled. I didn't need to see his face to know he was giving me a compliment.

I thanked them for all the books, and said, "Pablo's a little scared of his robot. He touches it with his paw and runs away." That made Grandpop laugh out loud.

Mom stayed in the guest room for a long conversation with Grandmary. Dad made Robot vacuum the living room during the conversation, so I didn't hear everything she said, but I knew she was talking about her recital.

By the time Zumu, Aunt Susan, and Uncle Eric arrived, the roast ducklings were sending out rich smells. Robot opened the door, and I told everyone where to hang their coats. Zumu had so many presents for me that Uncle Eric had to carry some of them and Dad had to go out to their car to get the rest. Robot placed the boxes carefully under the tree. The biggest box Zumu brought was very light and sort of swished when I shook it. What could it be?

I opened it first, and found a cherry red down jacket with lots of inside pockets.

"Your old one too small, and all stained," Zumu said when I thanked her. She pointed to another big, rectangular box. "Open that." It held a pair of tall dark red leather boots.

"They're beautiful!" I said, slipping on the jacket. The leather wallet fit neatly into one of the inside pockets. I could carry torsion wrenches and picks wherever I went.

"Now you'll never be locked in," Dad joked. Zumu shook her head, saying something loudly in Chinese. I knew she hadn't a clue why I would want to carry a lock-picking kit around.

I like all the food Mom makes for Christmas dinner, but the meal lasts way too long. When I asked to be excused, Zumu gave me her proudest smile and said something like "She is very polite" in Chinese.

While the grown-ups went on talking, I took the locks to my room and started working. Pablo sat on my desk to watch. I had disassembled one tumbler knob and reassembled it before Zumu, Aunt Susan, and Uncle Eric started back to Brookline.

I hugged Zumu before she went out the door. "See you in a week," I told her. "I love my new jacket."

That night in bed, in my clean, orderly room, with Robot's blue light pulsing softly beside me, I felt completely content. My room wasn't a mess any longer. I could find anything I wanted. Through my window, white lights decorating the Heartwright Estate shone on the snow. "All is calm, all is bright," I sang in my head.

As I drifted into sleep, I imagined what new pictures I could draw with the fifty-color box of felt-tip pens Mom and Dad had given me. They had come with a big white drawing pad, blank and as full of promise as the coming New Year.

14

Mom's Concert

The morning after Christmas, I woke to hear Mom playing nervous, rapid notes in the guest room. When I went to the kitchen to find some breakfast, I heard Dad moving around in his workshop, but I couldn't see him, because the door was closed. Mom had also closed the guest room door. I knew I didn't dare disturb her, so I fixed my own oatmeal, tiptoeing around the kitchen. Mom kept stopping and starting, sounding more and more frantic. A couple of hours later, she emerged to announce that she couldn't possibly go to Zumu's on New Year's Eve. "I'm not ready for the concert," she said. "I'll be up so late, when I could be practicing and resting." That made Dad really mad.

I was in my bedroom, working on the locks I got for Christmas, while Mom and Dad stood in the hall. Did they know I could hear every word? I concentrated on the cylinder and pick in front of me, trying to make a shear line by aligning the tumblers. But I couldn't block out their angry words. Dad exploded. "The *one* year you're free to go and you won't. Okay, have it your way. Don't go!"

"What about you? You work all the time! You never want to go out with anyone except your mother and people from work!"

I dropped the lock in frustration and covered my ears. Robot stood beside my bed. It could help me with the lock, but it couldn't stop my tears. I lay down beside Pablo, who was sleeping on my bed, took him in my arms, put my face in the fur on his neck, and let myself cry. He wriggled around and licked my cheeks. I wondered, as I had sometimes before, if Mom and Dad might ever get divorced. Compared to Jen's parents, they always seemed so tense and stressed. Would I have to choose between them? Would I like living with Dad and Robot? If I lived with Mom, who would take care of me when she was away?

Maybe practicing "The Swan" from *Carnival of the Animals* calmed Mom down. She planned it as an encore piece. "If I have an encore," she said. The music was certainly soothing, and by New Year's Eve, Mom and Dad had both relaxed a bit. Mom decided she could go to Zumu's after all. Dad said she didn't have to go, but you could tell by the tone of his voice that he wanted her to. I think she probably meant to go all along. Both of them say things they don't mean sometimes. I wish Robot could help me understand them as easily as it helped me clean out my closet.

The morning school started after the holidays, Dad told me not to tell anyone about my lock-picking tools, but I couldn't help showing them to Maeve and Jen. I'm sure they both thought I'd gotten a weird Christmas present, but they were too polite to tell me. Jen liked my jacket, though. I kept the tool wallet in my coat pocket in case I ever got locked out of someplace important.

Maeve wasn't very interested in clothes, but she and I had plenty of other things to talk about. As we rode the bus a week before Mom's recital, I told her how much Mom was practicing. She told me her mom and dad were really excited about going to the concert. They'd leave Maeve at home with her older sister, because they didn't want her to stay out so late on a school night.

"I'm going," I said. "But Mom and Dad want me to go to school the next day."

Tim, in the seat behind us, stuck his head forward and interrupted. "Are you going to leave your robot at home? How about I baby-sit it?"

Tim was so annoying.

Ever since school started after Christmas, Robot spent most of its time in my room on its charger. I didn't need it to open the door, since Mom was home every day after school. Some days, she gave me a hug and then went back to practicing her recital pieces. Other days, she waited for me at the bus stop. She always greeted Tim politely, and he was actually polite back, saying, "Hi there, Mrs. Chow," before he headed up the hill.

"It's hard for Maureen O'Mara," Mom said one afternoon as we walked up Heartwright Lane together, "working those crazy shifts at the hospital and trying to raise Tim on her own. I don't think she knows how much time he's spending up there. Mark certainly isn't the world's best influence."

Once dinner was over, Mom headed straight to the guest room and started playing her cello. As we cleaned up the kitchen, I bugged Dad to turn off Robot's reminders. "I don't really need them," I said. "I hardly even hear them anymore."

That weekend, Dad retreated to his workshop and took Robot with him. Through the half-open door, I could see him at his workstation, intent on his white laptop. When Dad finished, Robot still woke me up in the morning, and could still help me after school, but it wasn't so bossy. Dad fixed Robot so that I could disable some of its reminders with a voice command. Mom played the cello part of her Prokofiev opening duet over and over. While we put away dishes, Dad remarked, "It's the first time in years she's performed without Calyx. I think she's a little nervous."

A *little* nervous! The last week before her recital, Mom was out of her mind. She didn't hear what I was saying half the time. She forgot things. One day she forgot she'd promised to pick me up at school. I stood there waiting, worried that I'd gotten mixed up, wondering what to do. Eventually Mom drove up, rattled and apologetic. "When I got home from Charlotte's house, Robot reminded me," she explained. She imitated its synthesized tone: "The time is three-thirty and Celia has not arrived home from school."

We both laughed so hard we almost cried. It felt good to let everything out. Mom relaxed as we drove home.

"Should we dust off 'Dance of the Elves' in case I need another encore?" She wasn't really asking me. "That is," she said for the twentieth time, "if I play any encore at all."

"Of course you will," I told her. "Dad and Zumu and I will clap until you come out again."

She patted my knee with her free hand. "I hope the rest of the audience will agree with you."

Finally it was the night of Mom's recital. Dad told her that Pablo told him her music was perfect. I hugged her and said she would do great. She was actually smiling when Charlotte came to pick her up. I figured I'd better lay out my clothes for school so that I could pull them on fast next morning. I told Robot, "No alarm tomorrow. I don't need it. Dad's waking me up."

Dad and I ate a quick supper before we left. As we drove down Woodland Road, I could see lights through the drawn shades in Tim's house. I imagined him inside, watching some dumb television program.

Dad stopped at the florist for the roses he'd ordered, picked up Zumu in Brookline, and drove to MIT. He went to his favorite parking lot, down a narrow alley between a tall brick building and Omei, the Chinese restaurant Dad likes. Light shone through its windows. The smell of Chinese food filled the icy air. It made me hungry, even though I'd eaten already.

The smell got stronger as we walked back up the alley past a loading dock behind the brick building. Its big metal doors were shut tight. "Fisher's working late," Dad said, looking up at the lighted windows on the top floor. "Ultronics is the only one left in there. All the others went belly-up."

I looked up and tried to picture Christian Fisher in his office at Ultronics. I had never met him, so I had no idea if he was tall or short, fat or thin, ugly or good-looking. But I did find out what kind of car he drove when Dad pointed his chin toward a red sports car lightly dusted with snow and said, "I see he's still driving the same car."

Inside the hall, friends and neighbors smiled and waved at us as we walked to our front-row seats. I could tell Mom was nervous when she came out with Charlotte. Her eyes were kind of glassy and she wore that performer's smile. Everyone else probably thought she looked relaxed. Except Dad. His hand on the arm rest beside me was clenched into a fist. Mom and Charlotte looked at each other, nodded, and started to play. Dad opened his hand and let a out a deep breath.

I'd heard those long, low cello notes so often I thought I knew them by heart, but when the piano joined in, they sounded different. The cello and the piano were having a long conversation, using notes instead of words, sometimes pounding, sometimes flowing, sometimes picking. Mom stopped looking nervous and started to look the way she does when she goes far away inside the music. After Charlotte played the last thrumming notes, with Mom's cello weaving around them, everyone applauded loudly. As she and Charlotte took their bows, Mom seemed to see the audience for the first time. This time her smile was genuine.

Now Mom played her first solo piece, the one she'd been practicing the day she and Dad had that big argument. After the first notes, which always reminded me of someone scared, peeking around a corner, she slid into the melodic theme. When she finished, everyone applauded even more. Mom's recital was half over, and it was time for intermission. Dad said we shouldn't go backstage because it would break Mom's concentration.

We all stood in a little circle and talked with people we knew. Mr. Weissman turned up, wearing a suit that looked like he'd slept in it. I liked talking to Mr. Weissman, because he treated me like a grown-up. We talked about *Lord of the Rings,* which Mom and I had just finished. Dad glanced quickly at a small bearded man who stood inside a cluster of people, talking and smiling.

"That's the music critic for *The Boston Globe,*" Dad whispered to Mr. Weissman. I turned my head for a quick look at the man who would write the review of Mom's concert. Most kids don't even know what reviews are, let alone read them. In the paper, almost every week, people write about concerts or plays they've been to, and say whether they liked them or not and why. So what's the big deal? It's this: When Calyx gets a bad review, Mom's very upset. Sometimes she even cries. Then we have to stay out of her way. I guess it's like having the teacher make corrections in red all over your paper, giving you an F, and then showing it to everybody in school. People who read the bad review won't want your group to come and play in their town, so you lose money too.

I looked at the little man with the beard and wished very hard that he would like Mom's recital.

The lights blinked, signaling the end of intermission, and we went back to our seats. Mom's second solo piece would be music she loved best of all, Bach's unaccompanied "Cello Suite in D Minor." She looked a lot happier when she came on stage. She caught my eye and winked. Dad gave her a thumbs-up sign. She sounded really good, relaxed and flowing, as if the music were something she'd just thought of.

Charlotte came back, and they played the last piece together. It was modern music, and it marched and stomped as the piano and cello imitated each other, repeating passages of music. For a moment after the last notes died away, nobody clapped. Would Dad and I be the only ones? Dad lifted his hands, but before he could start, I heard loud applause behind me. I peeped around to see the short bearded man clapping sedately.

Mom seemed to smile at everyone while looking straight at me. Her excitement was like a great warm golden wave that flowed between us. The audience called her back for two encores. Finally she bowed some more and went away for good. At last we could go backstage. I carried Dad's bouquet of roses.

Mom laughed and hugged me, and then hugged and kissed Dad and Zumu. Then others crowded in. Dad loved all the attention. He joked, making everyone laugh. He called himself "the Star Cellist's Husband," and said, "The first solo didn't sound crummy at all." That was another pun, because the composer was named George Crumb.

Good thing Dad entertained people, because Mom's excitement seemed to carry her to some distant place, far away from us. She stared at a small woman with bright red lipstick, wearing a black hat, slowly weaving her way around Charlotte and her friends. I hadn't seen Madame Luczynski, Mom's old teacher, for a long time. She looked smaller and more frail than I remembered.

Mom reached out for her, and Madame took one of Mom's hands in both of hers. "My dear," she said, "that was superb. You have reached your stride as a soloist." She leaned close to Mom and spoke in a low voice. I heard her, because Mom had her arm around me, holding me close. She mumbled a name and position I didn't catch, ". . . the . . . chair in the Walden Chamber Orchestra will retire this summer. You should think about auditioning. You could tour alone, but you have other responsibilities."

I knew she meant me, because she stroked my hair and said, "You're growing up to be a little beauty."

Mom hugged her, and other people swept in and out. Then we all went to Omei for a late snack. Dad put his arm around Mom's shoulder as they walked ahead of me down the alley to our car. The pure white sheet of snow that had covered the loading dock earlier was mussed with footprints. The red car was gone. I could see tire tracks in the snow. Above my head, the windows on the third floor were dark. I was so sleepy that I was already half dreaming as I wondered why Mr. Fisher had come out across the loading dock instead of the street door. When we got in the car, Zumu and Dad in the front seats, Mom and I in the back, I fell fast asleep on Mom's shoulder. I never even heard Zumu leave the car.

A shrill, rhythmic scream shocked me awake. Our house alarm system.

Dad braked so abruptly that my seat belt pinched my waist. He leaped out of the car and ran up to the front door. By the time Mom and I got out of the backseat, Dad was rattling the front door. It wouldn't open, because the inside bolt had stayed in place. "They didn't make it!" Dad turned around, grinning. "They didn't get in!"

Just then a police car drove up. Dad entered the code, silencing the alarm, and opened the door to let us in. What a relief it was when the awful noise stopped! Snow dusted the trees and grass, and stars glittered in the sky. I'd never been out so late on a school night, and I wanted most of all to get in bed.

Pablo howled in the basement, upset by all the noise. I let him out and carried him into my bedroom. Robot stood in its place, recharging, its dome pale, rising and falling like the slow breathing of sleep. I could hear Dad and the policemen talking.

When Mom came in to kiss me good night and take Pablo away, she sounded tired but happy. She didn't look worried at all. "This has been some evening," she said.

"Do you think the robbers were after Robot?" I asked her.

"I don't think so," she said, stroking my hair. "Don't worry. The police think it was just some teenagers playing pranks."

After she left, as I drifted off to sleep, I remembered how much Tim wanted a robot. He'd been home and he knew we were gone. Had he tried to break into the house? As I wondered if I should tell Dad and the policemen, I sank into sleep for the second time that night.

15

Robot Gets a Locator

For the first time since my birthday, Robot didn't wake me up on a school day. Instead, Dad woke me up by touching my shoulder and whispering in my ear. We ate Morning Munch bars, standing in the kitchen, and I dressed quickly. "Mom will be up by the time you get off the bus," Dad told me. "She'll let you in, but I think you'll be too tired to do your homework." I was very glad I had laid out my clothes and school stuff before the concert.

Sitting beside Dad in the car as he drove along Woodland Road, I wondered if I should tell him about Robot's picture in the paper. If whoever tried to break in had seen that picture, it would be all my fault. But I was still scared that Dad would be angry and yell at me, so I talked about Tim instead.

"You know, Tim really wants a robot," I said to Dad. "Maybe he tried to break in. He knew we were at the concert."

Dad didn't answer right away. We had turned onto

School Street before he said, "I'm not worried about that kid. He's too dumb to crack my security system."

The late bell rang before I could say any more about Tim's threats.

Dad was right. All I wanted to do when I got home from school that day was curl up with Pablo under my comforter and sleep. The day had been raw and overcast, with snow spitting, and it was good to come home to a warm house with Mom at the door. She hugged me, looking tired but happy. Robot stood quietly on its recharger in my bedroom, issuing no reminders at all. When I woke up from my nap, I found Mom sitting at the breakfast bar in the kitchen reading *The Boston Globe* and smiling. There were bouquets of flowers in the vestibule and living room.

"What does it say?" I asked. She handed me the paper, folded open to show the review. The headline read, NEW TALENT DEBUT IN CAMBRIDGE. The review ran in columns around Mom's publicity photo, and it said lots of nice things and no bad things.

While I was reading, the phone rang. Grandmary and Grandpop were calling from Shandong. "It went very well," I heard Mom say. She told them what Madame Luczynski said, then listened for a while. "You're right," she answered, "but I'm still not sure I'm ready."

After she hung up, Dad called to say he had a project that would keep him late at work, so Mom fixed a cozy meal of soup in the kitchen and took the phone off the hook. "People have been calling all day," she said. "It's nice, but we need some quiet time."

Dad got home after I went to bed, and we all slept late on Saturday. After breakfast, Dad announced, "I'm going to work on Robot this weekend."

"What are you going to do?" I asked.

"Celia, it's complicated programming." Dad sounded impatient.

"Whatever you do, I want to help." I was pretty sure he wouldn't let me, but I wanted to see whatever he did to Robot.

"Alex," Mom said, "you gave that robot to her. At least let her watch."

Dad looked at me intently, as if I'd appeared out of nowhere. Otherwise, he didn't change expression. "Well, come on, let's get started," he said.

In his workshop, Dad really got into what he was doing. He heaved Robot onto his bench. Then he booted up the white laptop and started typing. He kept pushing up his glasses and squinting at the screen. Looking over his shoulder, I watched the green lines flicker and march up and out of sight. It was like looking at Chinese: A few strings of characters made sense, but most I didn't understand at all. Dad hooked his laptop to Robot's port and typed some more. The blue lights faded, the eyes retracted, the other lights went dark. Robot looked like it was sleeping.

"Caleb and I rigged up a transmitter." He showed me a small metal box, about the size of a deck of cards. "It's registered on a secure Moria website."

"What does it do?" I asked.

"If your robot gets lost, or if someone takes it, I can report it. Then the police can find it."

"How?"

"They have tracking computers set to the Global Positioning System. They bounce signals off satellites, so they're able to locate it, wherever it is."

"Could they find it at Tim's house?" I asked.

"Anywhere. Forget Tim," Dad answered absently, because he wasn't paying much attention to me. He was looking for something on his work table. "He'll never break into this house."

He pushed aside a pile of wires and found his special staple gun. "I'm more worried about scum like Christian Fisher. He'll bid on that recycling contract. Caleb and I have been watching Ultronics crank out prototypes for years. Some of them just look too much like Moria's. Fisher always claims that it's merely coincidence—says that since we're working on similar problems, we're coming up with similar solutions." Dad shook his head, clicking his tongue in irritation. "Caleb and I don't buy it. But we've never been able to prove he was stealing."

"You told me it's against the law to steal other people's ideas. Something about copyrights or—what's that other word?"

"Patents?" Dad turned Robot on its side.

I nodded.

Dad turned to look at me. His explanation came out in a rush. "To get a patent, you have to publish your idea, so other people can use it and improve on it. I don't want my idea made public. I meant to keep Robot secret until I sorted out its problems."

He picked up the transmitter, then spoke to me like I was his partner. "The idea is to put this where no one can see it. That way a thief won't know it's there."

"How about inside Robot's body?" I suggested. I thought Tim might not be able to find the locator if it was completely inside Robot.

"That's right. I'll have to partly disassemble Robot." He reached for a square-headed screwdriver.

"Dad, I can take screws out."

He looked as if he didn't quite believe me, but handed me the screwdriver. I tried to be super careful as I went to work on the screws that held Robot's disk to its base. Meanwhile, Dad rummaged around until he found a long, narrow scrap of plastic.

"I'll make a tunnel inside Robot to cover the locator. If I put some dead wires coming out, anyone who takes Robot apart might be fooled into thinking the covering is just a conduit for wires."

By this time I had taken out all the screws that held Robot to its base. Dad gently pulled the base away. I peered inside Robot's body. It was dark in there, but I could see clumps of wires going up to the dome, where they connected to the circuit boards, and down to the bottom, where they connected to the battery. The locator had adhesive on its back and a long wire dangling. Dad peeled off the paper covering and pressed it down inside Robot on the right side. He folded the long plastic strip to make flaps on both sides, attached three different-colored wires at the top, slid it up inside Robot so that it covered the locator, and reached in to staple it in place.

"Can I do the rest?" I asked.

He stopped and again looked straight at me, dubious. "You have to do it just right, or you could ruin your robot."

"Please? You can show me how."

He handed me the staple gun. "Hold it this way," he said. "No, that's wrong . . . there, that's right. Now don't press too hard. Be gentle. Don't rock the robot, or you'll damage it." And on and on. Eventually, I attached the plastic tunnel. I did it myself, and it wasn't nearly as complicated as Dad had predicted.

"Good," he said, without much expression. For Dad, that was high praise. Then he showed me how to connect the locator's wire to the battery.

"It will draw power from the battery," he said, "but it has its own backup." It felt good to do something all by myself, but I was glad that he reached in to make the dead wires look as if they were feeding into Robot's lens-eyes. I would have been scared to work so close to that miniature city of circuit boards.

Dad smoothed down his hair. His face relaxed. "That should fool any jerk who takes Robot apart."

I found the courage to ask, "Will you let me wake Robot up—I mean, boot up its program?"

Dad didn't answer, but he lifted Robot upright and gestured to the chair in front of his laptop. "Start with the

C key to turn on its power," he said. Patiently, step by step, he showed me how to reboot Robot.

Later, after Robot had made my bed and I had tidied my room, Dad told Mom and me the password we could use to log on to the locator website.

"Isn't this all far-fetched?" Mom said. "You've made this house so secure, and the robot never leaves the house. You've already closed the barn door, and the horse is still in the barn." Grandpop often repeated an old proverb about closing the barn door after the horse got away.

"This horse is one-of-a-kind," Dad said. "Better safe than sorry."

"An ounce of prevention is worth a pound of cure," I chimed in. Mom shook her head and started laughing. Dad and I laughed too. We were so tired and happy, all those old sayings sounded very funny.

Whenever I saw Tim on the school bus that week, I remembered the locator. Of course I couldn't tell him about it. Just try to steal Robot, I taunted him in my head.

A week or so later, the night before Calyx's five-day tour in the Midwest, Mom got a phone call from Lila. I hoped Lila would tell her the whole thing was off, but no such luck. After Mom hung up, she came into the living room, where Dad was reading the newspaper and I was curled up in a chair with Pablo purring against my chest, reading *The Dark Is Rising* for my book report.

"Remember Herb Goldman, that New York financier who doubled our fee last Thanksgiving?" she said. Dad looked up. "He's planning to propose on Valentine's Day, and he wants Calyx to play—to add to the romance."

Dad slammed the paper shut. "Ingrid, you know Caleb and I have an IT conference in Pittsburgh that Thursday and Friday. It's been on our calendar for months!"

Mom was all keyed up, more upset than I could remember. She yelled, which she doesn't usually do. "Can't you let Caleb go alone for once? The other three are dying for that fee."

Dad's face got all red. He threw the paper to the floor. "Can't you say no for once? I would give you your share of the fee to stay home."

"Why am I the one who has to refuse? You know how important my music is to me. You knew it when we got married, and when Celia was born. If I turn them down, I may have to leave the quartet!"

"Leave it then! I'm sick and tired of supporting your career with those neurotic women!"

"Just because you make more money doesn't mean your work is more important than mine!"

They seemed to have forgotten I was there. Something hard seemed to be growing inside my chest, cutting off my breath. I slammed my book down on the glass coffee table and stood up, tipping Pablo off my chest. He ran under the sofa. I took a deep breath, trying to shout. Instead, my voice came out all trembly.

"I'm old enough to take care of myself now! I don't even need Robot. You can lock it in your workroom. So stop arguing over who'll stay home with me!"

Mom closed her mouth and raised her chin. I could tell she was still very angry, although she spoke slowly and calmly. "Look, Alex, Celia would only be alone one night. Couldn't your mother stay with her?"

Dad folded up his newspaper. "She teaches every day. Remember?"

"She could come for the night and get back to her class the next day." Mom wrapped her arms around herself.

Dad's face was still flushed, but he had no expression, except that he was pressing his lips together very hard. That evening he was on the phone for nearly an hour, talking to Zumu in Chinese. I heard the English word *robot,* and *ta* which means "her" or "him," but I think Dad meant me. After he hung up, he said, "It's all arranged." He and Mom spent a lot of time discussing the plans he'd made. They sounded angry, but in the end they both seemed satisfied.

When the Calyx van drove up the next morning to take her to her flight to South Bend, Mom wasn't smiling. Her happy mood after the concert had evaporated. She hugged me, and just nodded to Dad. They both spoke in flat voices. I spent Saturday night while she was gone at Maeve's house. We did our favorite thing, acting out stories we had made up ourselves. That night we played "cork people" in her basement. Maeve's mom had saved a bag of corks, and we used markers to draw faces and clothes on them. We made a whole village. There was a war, a plague, and several murders. We jumped around, screaming and shouting and pretending to cry, and afterward I felt a whole lot better.

Mom came back from the Midwestern tour in a bad mood. The reviews were good, but the audiences were sparse, she said. I tried to cheer her up by saying how important good reviews are. Dad didn't say anything. When Jen and Maeve came over to make valentines, I don't think they noticed that Mom and Dad were hardly speaking.

Jen's mom had taken us to the craft store at East Haven Plaza, where we bought pink construction paper, red foil, doilies, stick-on hearts, glitter, glue—everything we needed. Mom spread newspapers over the oriental carpet in my bedroom, and then went off to the guest room to practice. We could hear her playing the romantic songs Mr. Goldman wanted. It wasn't hard music, but the cello went silent for long moments, and then started up half-heartedly.

I showed Robot how to draw around several heart templates. It kept drawing hearts in different sizes and shades of pink and red for us to cut out. Sitting on the floor of my bedroom, we used markers, doilies, and glitter to decorate our valentines, fancy ones for our parents, then simple ones for every person in the class. Jen thought it was mean to leave anyone out, even the boys. Somehow, Robot had a list of all the kids in our class. As it recited names, we checked off our valentines.

I decorated a valentine for Pablo, punched a hole in the top, and tied it around his neck with a red ribbon. He put his ears back and switched his tail and paced around my room, looking very annoyed, which made us all giggle. He was relieved when I took it off. Robot vacuumed the carpet after we tidied up. By now I was used to having a robot housekeeper, but Jen and Maeve were fascinated.

Mom and Dad and Zumu spent a lot of time planning that Valentine's Day, down to the last detail. Dad came back from the lab Tuesday night with a long printed sheet full of lists and instructions: the flight plan for the jet they were renting, contacts for him in Pittsburgh, the phone number of the limousine company that was taking Mom to New York, his cell phone number, and Mr. Goldman's phone number.

"Honestly, Alex," Mom said, "I'll call home whenever I can. We'll be practicing most of the day. All those love songs!" Her voice dripped with scorn. She didn't approve of Mr. Goldman's choice of music. "Rogers and Foster are all right," she muttered, "but that soft rock makes me feel like I'm playing elevator music!"

Dad ignored her. "Celia, Zumu will drive over after her class. She should be here before you get home from school. Robot will see you off and lock the door after you, just like it does when Mom's on tour."

Mom didn't say anything. I knew she never liked the idea of a robot baby-sitter, but there was really no one else she trusted to take care of me.

Dad checked and rechecked all the windows to make sure they were locked. He went over his instructions to me several times. "Don't turn off the radio. It's on a timer. Be sure to lock the basement door after you put Pablo down." Dad seemed more worried about keeping the house safe than about keeping me safe.

Nobody spoke much Wednesday night. Mom and Dad were busy packing, and I was making one last valentine—for Robot. I cut out a big red heart and a smaller pink one and glued them together. I cut my last doily to make a narrow lace border. Then I glued sparkles outlining the pink heart and wrote in the middle, *Celia loves Robot.* I got some really strong double-stick squares, the kind Mom uses to hang things sometimes, and pressed one side against the valentine. I would give it to Robot in the morning.

16

On My Own

It seemed like the middle of the night when Mom came in to kiss me good-bye. She had let Pablo out of the basement. He nosed down under my covers.

"The limo's waiting," Mom whispered. "I hate to leave you again." She smoothed back my hair. "I wish I didn't have to play at this party. It isn't the money. I just can't let the others down."

She rubbed her cheek against my temple, lightly kissing my hair. "I'll call at three, when you're home from school."

Through my closed door, I heard Dad rumble, "Why wake her up? Let her sleep."

Pablo turned around to arrange himself next to my stomach, purring and kneading. The next thing I knew, Dad was rubbing my shoulder.

"Almost time to get up," he said. "I have to leave for the airport now. It's overcast, but they've cleared our pilot for takeoff. Robot will tell you what to do."

I'm sure it will, I thought.

I heard the garage door open and close as Dad's car backed out. The noise died away, and I knew he was turning onto Woodland Road. Mom and Dad were zooming off in opposite directions, leaving me all alone.

As Robot played its cheerful melody, I told myself that when I got home from school, I'd be able to tell Zumu about our class Valentine's party, and Mom too, when she called me. I tried to look forward to the party, but I kept remembering the break-in. All Robot's chatter couldn't fill up the empty hole inside my chest. I felt lonely and scared. Mom and Dad were going so far away from me.

"Today will be overcast, with a high of thirty degrees Fahrenheit, and a chance of snow," Robot said. It helped me lay things out and gave precise instructions for making cocoa and oatmeal. I didn't remind it that I already knew how. It did most of the cleaning up. I put Pablo back in the basement. He had a cozy bed there, and Dad had rigged a heating pad with its own thermostat, so he'd always be warm.

I left valentines for Mom and Dad on their bedroom dressers. I was really glad I had Robot. Even though I had told Mom and Dad I could take care of myself, I needed Robot's company more than its help.

Robot stood in the vestibule with its usual list of reminders, which had become automatic by now, but it added one more. "Today is Valentine's Day. There will be a party in your classroom. Do not forget the valentines you have made."

"They're in my backpack. And here's one for you."

I stripped the backing off and pressed Robot's valentine against a smooth spot on its front, right near where its heart would be. I knew I would have to use some awful solvent to get it off, but I'd worry about that later. Right then, it looked great.

Robot swiveled its camcorder eyes, trying to see what I had pasted on it. "Thank you, Celia," it said. "This decoration is appropriate." I felt my throat tighten, almost as if I was about to cry. With Mom and Dad gone, Robot was the only family I had.

Robot went back to doing its job. It opened the closet near the front door to pluck out my red boots, dangling one from each hand. I sat on the bench and pulled them on. Then it held out the down jacket Zumu had given me for Christmas, and after that, my hat, muffler, and mittens. "Proper foot and head protection will be necessary today," it chirped.

"Bye, Robot," I said. "Be nice to Zumu. See you this afternoon." I closed the front door, knowing Robot would activate the security system and roll back to my bedroom until it was time for me to come home. I had left my room tidy, the kitchen clean. All my homework was up to date. Robot had taught me a lot since my birthday, but it couldn't make up for that empty feeling of missing Mom and Dad.

Outside, damp, chilly air stung my hands and cheeks. I put on my mittens and tightened my muffler as I walked down Heartwright Lane to the bus stop.

"Smells like snow," Mrs. Flynt commented as I climbed up the steps of the school bus. I settled in a seat, but the bus didn't move. Mrs. Flynt looked back at me in her mirror. "Where's Tim today?" she asked. We could both see lights in his house.

"Don't know," I mumbled. I didn't add, "Don't care," because I knew Mrs. Flynt liked Tim. He was probably pretending to be home sick. Maybe he wanted to avoid Valentine's Day at school. Who would give him a valentine?

Minutes passed while the bus idled. At last, Mrs. Flynt drove on. I sighed with relief and settled back for a peaceful ride, watching trees and houses glide by. Cars streamed past us. I saw Jude driving the blue van up Woodland Road, heading for the Heartwright Estate. Then we came to Maeve's stop. When she sat next to me, I told her how Robot "looked" at its valentine.

A few snowflakes swirled down as we walked across the schoolyard. Through our classroom windows, I watched snow fall, thicker and faster, until it covered the playground, piling like frosting on the basketball hoops and tree branches. At morning recess, you couldn't see across the playground. A cold wind blew snow in our faces. Maeve and Jennifer and I started a snowman. My mittens got soaked, but I didn't mind. I liked the icy crunch of snow against my hands as we mounded up the body.

We slogged through mounting drifts on our way back from recess. It took us a long time to get settled, what with taking off our boots and mittens and hanging up our coats and wondering whether school would let out early. Once we took our seats, Mrs. Flower announced that we would start the Valentine's party.

Jen and Roger Ennis passed out valentines. Last week, our class had decorated the big box to hold them. A few kids had dropped valentines in early, but most had stuffed theirs in the box that morning, just like me. I opened each valentine as soon as Jen or Roger put it on my desk.

Some were store-bought and pretty unoriginal. That's what happens when you bring valentines for everyone in the class. I got some nice ones, but I forgot them because of the last valentine. Jen dropped a big white envelope on my desk. "It was on the bottom of the box," she said. "Someone must have put it in last week."

I was glad she went back to her desk to open her own valentines, because I didn't want her or anyone else to see this one. My name was printed in a boy's writing. I think I knew who it was right then, but I didn't want to admit it. I almost didn't open it, but I couldn't stop my fingers. Inside I found a piece of construction paper folded over with a cartoon drawing on the front, an ugly stick figure of a girl with slanty eyes and black pigtails standing beside a black canister that had to be Robot. Inside a verse was hand printed:

> Celia is selfish
> Celia is mean
> Celia can't keep Robot
> That's plain to be seen.

I scrunched it up in a ball and pushed it into my desk.

"Who's your secret valentine?" Maeve came up to my desk to check out my cards.

"No one," I said. "It was a joke, but it wasn't very funny." I was surprised to find myself choking back angry tears.

Then the party started. Our room mother had brought juice and heart-shaped cookies. When I was in kindergarten and first grade, I wished that Mom would be room mother, but she was always too busy. Now that I'm older, I'd be embarrassed to have her come to class.

I'd just taken my first sip of juice when the lights in our classroom flickered and went out. The classroom was already noisy because of the party, but now everyone started making noise at once. One of the boys behind me yelled something dumb, like, "The lights are out!" and others just grunted or cheered.

"Stay in your seats," Mrs. Flower commanded. "We can always recite the times tables, lights or not." We groaned, but quieted down. Mr. Lyman appeared at our door. We watched as he spoke quietly to Mrs. Flower. She asked a question or two. Then he left.

"Class," she announced. "The power is out all over West Haven. They think a tree fell down under the weight of the snow and hit a transformer. School will be dismissed in half an hour, while the buses can still get through. Mrs. Ketchum and the teacher aides are calling your homes now. If someone is there, you will be dismissed. If not, you will go to the cafeteria for group study hall."

I looked at Maeve and Jennifer. Both their moms would be home, I was sure. I didn't want to stay at school without them. Yet I knew I shouldn't go home with either one of them, because Zumu would be coming and Mom had promised to call. So I raised my hand. "Mrs. Flower, my robot is home. It can't answer the telephone, but Dad leaves me with it all the time. My grandmother will be there later. Can I go?"

She nodded, distracted. I'm not quite sure she heard me. I could see that she wanted to get as many children as possible out of her classroom.

Maeve and I walked across the schoolyard, taking big steps in our boots, skidding and struggling and giggling, supporting each other through snowdrifts, until we reached the bus, which was waiting on the street behind the school. Mrs. Flynt had her windshield wipers on high, and you could hear their whining rhythm—*rurra-rurra, rurra-rurra, rurra-rurra*—all over the bus. Cars crawled along in slow motion, sending up sprays of dirty snow. A blue van on the other side of the road started forward toward the bus while it let kids off, but Mrs. Flynt honked and it stopped. I looked down to see a puffy face under a blue stocking cap and scraggly hair pulled back in a ponytail. Jude sure hadn't stayed long at the Heartwright Estate. He was probably heading home to hole up out of the storm.

When I got off the bus, I could still see lights on in Tim's house. Slipping and sliding up Heartwright Lane through snow halfway to the tops of my red boots, I decided he'd picked a good day to skip school. My backpack was all soggy with snow by the time I made it to the door. Then it dawned on me that if the electricity was off, the security system wouldn't be working. For the first time I worried about Robot. What would happen if it tried to connect with a switched-off security system?

In a panic, I pushed on the door, not sure it would open. As it swung inward, I almost fell into the house. Robot was not there to greet me.

I noticed a strange smell first, something like burning rubber mixed with the odor of a sweaty body. Then I saw a puddle of water on the entry hall.

My heart began to beat so hard, it shook my whole body. I could hardly breathe. Dad had always told me that if I came home and the security system was down, I shouldn't go inside because a burglar might still be there. I knew I should run out of the house, but I didn't know where to go. Besides, I had to find Robot and check on Pablo. I wouldn't say I was thinking very well, but somehow I knew I had to find Robot first.

I put my backpack down as quietly as I could and pulled off my boots, balancing against the wall. I'd make less noise in my stocking feet. I left the front door open and tiptoed to the kitchen. No one there, or in the living room. Everything looked the same, except darker, more shadowy.

The silence was spooky. No refrigerator hum, no heating noises. I walked as quietly as I could down the hall, past the potted avocado. No one was in the TV room or the guest room. I was too scared to look in the closets. What if someone had hidden there?

Holding my breath, afraid the sound of my heart beating would echo through the house, I slid along the wall, heading for my bedroom. In the dim, watery light coming from my windows, it looked just as I had left it that morning: bed neatly made, nightgown and robe hung up in the closet, dirty clothes in the hamper, desk and floor tidy, papers and books stored where they should be.

Raggedy Ann stared at me with her shoe-button eyes and perpetual smile. Beside my bed, the charger sat empty, forlorn and useless. I stared at it, feeling a shock of horror. I knew then that Robot was gone, but I didn't want to admit it, so I kept looking, thinking maybe I would find it in another room.

I tiptoed across the hall into Mom and Dad's bedroom, and even looked in their bathroom. I opened the door to their closet. Mom's heavy robe hung there. I plunged my face into it, smelling the delicate spicy powder she used, and felt tears start. I wanted Mom and Dad so much at that moment. I rubbed away tears with the back of my hand, but they kept running down my cheeks.

Then I saw the worst thing. The door to Dad's workshop was slightly ajar. His electronic lock had failed. I pushed the door with my fingertips, still not quite ready to believe that it would open. Every inch of Dad's workbench was littered with stuff, except the clear spot where the white laptop had been. The laptop he had used to program Robot. Then I realized that whoever left the puddle in the entry hall had come into the house when the power went down, planning to steal Dad's prototype.

I stumbled back to the kitchen, still crying, and heard Pablo meowing through the basement door. When I opened it, he jumped into my arms, licking tears off my face. He had a lot to say, too. He meowed urgently, as if trying to tell me what had happened. "I wish I could understand you," I whispered.

I picked up the phone to call Dad's cell phone. But the line was dead. Of course. Every phone in the house was cordless. Without electricity, they wouldn't work. I wished then, for the hundredth time, that I had a cell phone.

Wishing wouldn't help. I was on my own, and I knew this much for sure: Dad's robot was gone. His own invention, the one he was so proud of. The robot that had changed my life. I felt responsible for it, and I knew I had to get it back. It and the laptop.

At the same moment, I remembered who had threatened to steal Robot. Who hadn't been in school that day. Who had sent me that awful valentine.

I was so angry I hardly thought. I rubbed Pablo's head and set him on the basement stair. "I'll be back later!" I told him as I quickly closed the door. He replied with a frustrated howl.

I pulled my boots on, slid into my jacket, and ran down Heartwright Lane in the blowing snow, taking big jumping steps and gasping for air, but forcing myself to go faster. One car moved slowly along Woodland Road, the sound of its engine muffled. After that, silence. No distant motors. Certainly no snowplow.

When I reached Tim's house, I was completely out of breath. I pounded on the door so hard I almost fell through when it opened. There stood Tim, wearing an old sweatshirt and blue jeans, staring at me as if I had dropped down from another planet.

"Timothy O'Mara!" I couldn't yell very loud because I was panting and crying, but I did the best I could. "You give me back my robot!"

17

The Surprise at Tim's House

Tim backed into his house. He looked scared. I was so sure I'd find Robot that I charged right in and started exploring.

He stood there staring at me for a long time before he finally said something. "What are you talking about?" he stammered, sounding very confused. When I started toward his living room, his voice got stronger. "Take off your boots," he ordered. "My mom doesn't like snow on the carpet."

It was an ugly carpet, pale orange and glossy. But Tim sounded so much like Dad and Robot that I heeled out of my boots. If I thought about it at all, I thought that Mrs. O'Mara probably had enough trouble with Tim as a son. She didn't need snow on her carpet too. The house was much neater than ours. Too neat. It was uncomfortable, like a doctor's office waiting room.

I threw my boots back by the front door, which still stood open. The cold air made my wet stockings feel icy against my feet. "Don't act so innocent." I caught my breath and pushed back tears, and my voice came out louder and stronger. "You couldn't even figure out how to break the security system. You had to wait until the power went out."

A strange expression came over Tim's face. He looked frightened, but he sounded angry. "Liar, liar, stuck-up liar!"

He stomped around me and slammed the front door closed. "You made this all up to blame me!" he yelled. "Look around the house for yourself. You won't find—"

I didn't let him finish what he was going to say. I marched into his living room and looked behind the sofa and chair. They were covered in some gross flowered fabric that didn't match. Lace doilies were draped over the back and arms of each. There wasn't a speck of dust or dirt anywhere. I peered behind the dark television. No robot. No laptop.

I toured the other rooms of the house. His mother's room had a light in the shape of the Virgin Mary, above a bed covered by a worn chenille bedspread. Tim's room was tiny and dark, with a battered desk. Sitting on the desk was something that surprised me: my old Mind-Mate. I opened my mouth to say, "So you were the one who bought my MindMate!" but I closed it before the words came out. I felt as if I'd bumped against a hard wall, with my breath knocked out of me. I didn't know what to do with my face. I stared at the library books on his desk and the *Star Wars* posters on the wall. A Red Sox baseball cap, like the one I threw away, hung on top of a bat leaning against the wall. I had to admit that his room was neater than mine ever was before Robot took charge. Tim didn't have enough stuff to be messy. What would it be like, I wondered, to want a new computer and have to buy a used one, especially one as old as the MindMate?

I was beginning to wish I'd never come. With elaborate courtesy, Tim opened the bathroom for me to look in. Clean but dingy and old. No robot. No laptop.

It was Tim's turn to taunt me. "Didn't find him, did you? That's because he's not here! Did you ever think how I'd move Robot from your house? Do you think I could press a button and roll him over the snow?"

I put my hand over my mouth to cover a gasp. Tears stung in my eyes, and I couldn't answer while I tried to swallow them. "After you sent me that awful valentine, I was sure you . . ." I couldn't finish. I swallowed hard and started again. "It had to be someone with a car."

You can imagine how embarrassed I felt. I turned to leave. I wanted to get out of there as fast as I could.

Tim followed me to the door. "You made me so mad when you wouldn't talk to me about your robot. You with your rich dad who gives you everything. I just wanted to tease you to get even."

I didn't want to talk to Tim anymore. I wanted to run home. But my boots took longer to put on than take off.

"I don't believe your robot's even gone. I bet your dad took him back to Cambridge!"

There was no bench by their door. It's hard to pull boots on standing up, especially if you're trying to look dignified.

"I looked all over my house. It's not there!" My words came out as a whiny wail. "Dad's lab was wide open. Someone must have stolen Robot. The thief left puddles on the floor and I can smell him in the house. Dad's in Pittsburgh, and Mom's in New York. My grandmother was supposed to come over this afternoon, but I don't know if she can get here in the storm." I couldn't keep control of my voice, so my last words sounded really hysterical. "And none of our phones work."

Tim's face got all red. "Our phone is fine," he stammered. "Why don't you call the police?"

His phone, an antique rotary, was mounted on a wall next to the front door. Mrs. O'Mara had printed emergency numbers on a card taped beside it. My hand shook, so it was hard to dial. "Somebody's stolen my robot!" I yelled at the woman who answered.

"Are your parents available?" she asked.

"No, but I have the locator password. You go to the Moria Systems website—"

The woman cut me off. "Honey, all our officers are out in the snow emergency. The power's out all over town. We don't have time to take care of a stolen toy. Have your parents call when they get home, and we'll file a report." With that, she hung up.

I was angry and humiliated. I slammed down the

phone and dialed Dad's cell phone. He didn't answer, and I was too scared to leave a message, so I hung up and went back to putting on my boots.

"What did they say?" Tim asked.

"They think I'm just a kid who's lost a toy." I spit the words out, trying to balance on one foot. "Dad's cell phone is off."

"So now what are you going to do?" he asked.

"I don't know." This time I couldn't hold back my tears or keep my balance. I collapsed in a heap beside Tim's front door. "Robot's gone and so is Dad's laptop with all his secret programs. Dad will blame me, I know he will!"

"It wasn't your fault the power went out," Tim said. "Look, you're all upset. You can't even think straight. I'm making lunch. Want some?"

I stared at him, my mouth hanging open, I was so astonished. He actually sounded almost . . . kind. Suddenly, I hated the idea of slogging back through the snow to my cold empty house, a house that still smelled of a burglar. I pulled off the one boot I'd managed to put on, took off my down jacket and hung it on the doorknob, and padded into the kitchen.

"Sit down," Tim said, pointing to a chair at the kitchen table. He poured the rest of a can of tomato soup into the saucepan heating on the stove, added a little more milk, and gave it a stir. Luckily he had a gas stove, like us, so he could cook when the lights went out. Then he pulled out four slices of a kind of bread I'd heard Mom call "white rubber," and slapped them down on the kitchen counter.

"Your robot didn't walk off by himself. Somebody did steal him. Somebody who knew you had to take a laptop, too. I wouldn't have thought of that." Tim opened the refrigerator and took out a package of baloney, a jar of mayonnaise, and a head of lettuce, the really crunchy kind called iceberg that Mom will never buy.

Then I really knew how stupid I'd been, to think Tim had stolen the robot.

"Of course!" I shouted. "It had to be that Christian Fisher Dad's always talking about."

"Who's he?" asked Tim. I explained to him about Robot's vision and how Dad was making a secret prototype, one that could learn things from a person. How he'd given his prototype to me in place of a baby-sitter so he could watch its performance. I told him about the attempted break-in after Mom's concert. While he listened, he made baloney sandwiches.

Why hadn't I figured this out before I'd accused Tim? It was all so obvious. My words followed my thoughts and came out in a tumbling rush. "That picture in *The Villager*. He must have seen it somehow. You know, when I took Robot to school and it rescued a kitten? Dad was so worried that someone would find out what he'd done with vision if they knew that a robot could tell the difference between a cat and a dog."

Tim had stopped cutting the sandwiches. After a moment he started again, cutting them in half and handing me one on a piece of paper towel. He poured soup in two mugs and gave me one. He didn't meet my eyes.

"He had to know whose kid I am. There aren't any other Chinese girls at Abigail Adams," I babbled on.

I wrapped my hands around the mug of soup to get warm. "You weren't in school today. Another reason I suspected you. Were you here this morning?"

"Mom works the early shift, so I called in sick," he said, as if cutting school was the most normal thing in the world. Tim sat down with me but glanced away, out the kitchen window. His voice shook a little.

"I thought I'd go up to the Heartwright place to shovel snow and earn some money. But Mark called me early and told me not to come. I guess he didn't need me, because he had Jude to help him. I saw his blue van turn up Heartwright Lane. I didn't see it come out, though. I was mostly watching TV after that—until the power went out."

I banged my mug down. "That van met the school bus on Woodland Road—before our stop. The guy you call Jude was driving. "

Tim finally turned to look at me. He was wearing a weird expression.

"Jude asked me a lot of questions about Robot," Tim said slowly. "He was really, really interested."

Suddenly it all made sense.

"He's been hanging around our house," I said. "Spying on us, watching for his chance! Calling himself Jude."

I stood up. I was beginning to make a plan. "Thanks for lunch, Tim," I said.

"You haven't finished," he protested. "Where are you going?"

"To Fisher's lab, of course. Robot's got to be there."

"Are you crazy? How're you going to get there?"

"On the T. I've done it with Dad dozens of times. Fisher works near the Chinese restaurant where we go all the time."

"You're going to go knock on his door and ask him nicely to give back your robot? And, hey, by the way, that laptop, too?" Tim's voice dripped with scorn.

The way he said it made me sound so dumb. I sat back down.

"If Jude is Fisher in disguise, he's a *criminal*," Tim said. "You should call the police again."

I wiped up the soup I'd spilled, drank some, and took a few bites of my sandwich. "I don't want to waste time waiting for Dad, or for the cops. They won't listen to me anyway. I've got to find Robot before Fisher takes it apart. Dad put in a locator. If Fisher disables it, he could take Robot anywhere. I've got to find Robot. And the laptop. *Then* I'll call the police."

Tim's mouth tightened. I'd never seen him look like that. Horrified? I kept talking. "If I go home and my grandmother's there, she'll just make me wait for Dad. If I do that, they'll have time to figure everything out. They'll steal Dad's ideas. I've got to try to stop them!"

"No way!" Tim said. I think he meant he understood. He tilted his mug and sipped the last of his soup. He stood up, put his mug in the sink, and ran water into it. "But you can't do it alone. They'd recognize you right away. I could be any kid with nothing to do on a snow day. That's why I'm going with you."

I stared at him, more astonished than ever. "It's not *your* robot," I stammered.

"I know, but I've always wished he was mine, you know. After you brought your robot to school, Jude wanted to know everything about him. That was fine with me. I wanted to talk about Robot. I kept blabbing . . ." Tim sounded as if he might cry. He took a deep breath.

"He told me to sit behind you on the bus. He told me what questions to ask you. So in a way, I did help steal him. But I didn't know . . ." He turned around and looked down at the sink, mumbling, so I could hardly hear him. "I'd like to help you get him back."

I did some more protesting and Tim argued with me but in the end it was settled. Tim made me explain exactly what I planned to do. I had forgotten that Dad always drove to the T stop and parked the car there. We decided against calling a taxi because Tim said his mother did it when their car broke down and it never came. He thought we should take the bus.

I showed him a map in the telephone book and

explained how we'd have to change to the Red Line at Park Street Station. I told him where we'd have to get off. He called the T's emergency number to make sure the trains were still running. They were.

Tim bundled up and I put on my jacket and boots. I patted my locksmith tools, thinking I might need them. Tim locked the door behind us and we walked up Heartwright Lane. When Tim saw a bus coming down Woodland Road, he yelled and waved his arms, and it slowly came to a stop. It was almost empty.

"Thanks, Mr. Drummond," Tim said, panting, as he dropped in his money.

"What brings you out on a day like this?" The driver seemed like an old friend of Tim's. He stared at me, registering my Chinese face. I'd seen the bus go along Woodland Road, but I had never taken it.

Tim threw himself into an empty seat near the front. I sat in the next seat down and tried to look inconspicuous. "School's out," Tim said. "Snow day. We're heading for the science museum."

"You be careful in all this snow," Mr. Drummond said. "Try to stay dry and warm."

"We'll be careful," Tim promised.

A train was pulling in just as we reached the stop, which was lucky, because they were probably running slower than usual in the storm. We ran to catch it. There was no time to think.

It wasn't until we were sitting in the rattling, swaying train, watching houses and trees glide by, veiled in falling snow, that I remembered I'd left the house door open. When Zumu got there, she'd go crazy. She'd call Dad on her cell phone right away. Would she let Pablo out of the basement? And what would she say when Mom called?

18

A Torn Heart

Tim followed me out of the stop for MIT. Climbing was treacherous, because dirty slush made the stairs slippery. Heavy snow had stopped falling. Only a few scattered white flakes drifted lazily down. I found my way through a maze of streets between the T stop and the restaurant. The main roads were clear, but snowplows hadn't touched the sidewalks and smaller side streets. Sometimes we had to climb over drifts of packed snow. When I fell, Tim helped me up, and when he fell, I grabbed his arm to pull him up.

"There's Omei." I'm not sure why I whispered. I breathed in the cold damp air with relief. I'd never been quite sure that I could find Ultronics. At the same time, I was scared, being so close to the thieves. My legs felt weak and unsteady.

The sign on Omei's door said Closed. Its neon sign wasn't glowing. Through the windows I could see empty tables, with their white tablecloths and teacups sitting upside down, waiting for people to come and eat.

"That's where he works." I pointed up. A huge

mound of snow blocked the alley leading to the lot where we had parked the night of Mom's concert. I wished we could walk down the alley to look for lights on the top floor, but we couldn't. Even if the big mound hadn't blocked our way, the alley was so clogged with snow, we would have had to dig our way through it. Mr. Fisher's red car would be completely buried. Tim reached into the cold mound with his mittened hand. He scooped away snow to reveal blue metal.

"His van," I whispered.

Tim dug away more snow until he uncovered the license plate. "ELY 722," he whispered. "That's Jude's van, all right."

Fisher's van, I corrected in my mind.

We headed toward the double doors of the building. Tim got there first and pushed one. It wasn't locked. Slowly, we tiptoed inside.

We found ourselves in a lobby, facing an elevator. Dim lights glowed from the ceiling.

"Boston has power," Tim whispered.

Beside the elevator was a glass-covered directory, the kind with a black background and slots for white letters you could move around or take in and out. Most of the slots were empty, or had one or two forlorn letters hanging askew, not spelling anything. But the bottom slot held a line that made sense: Ultronics 3

"Dad said there used to be more companies in this building," I muttered to Tim.

The lobby wasn't very warm, but it was warmer than

the street. In spite of that, a chill starting just under my heart spread to the tips of my toes, making me feel cold all over. I'd been so angry and brave at Tim's house, but as we got closer and closer to our destination, I felt my courage leaking away like air from a balloon. I don't know what I would have done if I'd been by myself. The thought of Robot, up there somewhere, all alone, maybe torn apart, made me want to rescue it. But mostly I kept going because I didn't want Tim to see how scared I was.

I hated the thought of being locked up in that elevator inside an empty building. On the wall beside the directory, close to the corner of the lobby, there was a door marked by a bright red Exit sign. I walked over and pulled it open. Sure enough, stairs led up. We climbed them. Quietly.

When we got to the second floor, I opened the door to peer down a long hallway. Fluorescent ceiling bulbs flickered and sputtered. There was hardly enough light to see the offices opening onto the corridor. A few empty cartons were stacked on the dusty hall carpet.

Tim pulled me back into the stairwell and we started up again. My boots seemed to weigh a ton. They had been soaked by the snow, and now I could feel water seeping through my socks and squishing as I stepped.

The third floor had a corridor just like the second, with a dusty carpet and flickering fluorescent bulbs. An office near the middle of the corridor, on the right, seemed to give off light from inside. Carefully and quietly, Tim closed the stairwell door behind us. Slowly, we made our way toward that office. Sure enough, etched on a big glass door was the word *Ultronics.*

Through the glass wall beside the door we could see a long room, separated by a partition. An empty receptionist's desk faced the door. The partition separated it from a long room divided into cubicles. There wasn't a person in sight. I pulled gently and the glass door swung open. Behind the receptionist's desk, another door stood half open.

Slowly, cautiously . . . that's how we moved, until we heard muffled footsteps. Someone. Coming from the back office. Coming toward us. Those footsteps seemed to echo like thunder in the silence. Then we scooted, fast and scared, into the long room and ducked down inside a far cubicle.

We heard someone walk around the receptionist's desk, heard the glass door creak as the person left the office. I stood up and peered over the cubicle wall. Through the glass, I could see the back of a big man with a long greasy ponytail, heading down the corridor. Even though I couldn't see his face, I knew he was Fisher, alias Jude. He was about the same shape, and he had the same color shirt. I could just see him down the hallway as he stood waiting for the elevator. It came up, and he stepped on.

"I bet Jude's going out for pizza," Tim whispered. "He lives on pizza."

"Fisher," I whispered, correcting Tim out loud this time. "Who knows how long he'll be gone? Come on."

We headed through the open door behind the receptionist's desk and found ourselves in another corridor. A square of light fell on the carpet ahead, shining from yet another open door. We were still trying to walk quietly, even though we had Ultronics to ourselves, and the carpet helped. Tim started down the corridor, but I stopped and grabbed his arm.

On the floor were ragged pieces of red and pink paper and shreds of lace. Parts of Robot's valentine. My own heart seemed to stop, and tears prickled behind my eyes. I was furious and sad, all at once. "I put this on Robot this morning," I whispered. "Fisher must have torn it off."

"Maybe he wasn't alone," Tim whispered. "Don't make any noise."

We kept close to the wall. I was the first one to peer around the door frame into the lighted room. I saw a big, high-ceilinged lab with black-topped electrical benches along the wall and two more in the center. On the closest center bench lay Robot.

Only it wasn't Robot anymore. Its clear plastic dome had been pried off and tossed aside. Its camcorder eyes dangled from wires down over its canister body. The blinking blue light had gone dark. Its plastic body had been cut open. Its little monitor and keyboard had been gouged out of its body and thrown on the bench beside it. Circuit boards and wires spilled out of the hole; scattered buttons littered the workbench. Dismembered plastic arms sprawled on the table.

My stomach turned over, it was so gruesome. I felt

like throwing up, like I did when I found the Levins' cats after Rocky killed them.

Tim peered over my shoulder. When I heard his gasp, I turned my head to look at him. You read about people turning white, but I'd never seen someone actually do it. Without thinking, I pushed him back, away from the door, against the wall, using all my strength.

"Listen." I spoke in his ear, keeping my voice low. "He didn't cut into Robot's side. I've got to make sure the locator's still there, and connected to the battery."

Tim looked so shocked that I wasn't sure he heard me. I grabbed his arm and held on tight. I didn't think it out, but somehow I knew he had to do something or he'd fall apart.

"We don't know when Fisher's coming back." I wanted to yell at him, but I was so scared I kept whispering. "I'll fix the locator and try to find Dad's laptop." I nodded at the lab door. "You go back down to the office and watch for him. You can hide behind the big desk. There's a phone there. Try to call for help. If you see the elevator light, run back here and warn me. Then we'll have time to hide."

Tim didn't answer. He only nodded.

"Don't worry about Robot." I was still whispering. "It's not alive. It's not like a pet. Dad can fix it, good as new." I turned around and went into the big lab.

It's only a machine, I told myself as I stepped from the carpeted hallway to the hard floor tiles. Even though there was no one to hear my boots squishing across the lab floor, I tried to walk as quietly as I could. It's only a machine, I told myself again. It's not alive, like Pablo.

The lab was empty, but there was a door on the far side, open a crack. Probably a small office off the lab, I thought. I turned my back on the door and forgot all about it as I made my way around the lab bench, slowly, carefully, quietly. All I could think of was Robot, dismembered and useless.

Shredded remnants of the valentine were still stuck to the ripped cylinder that had been Robot's body. The black plastic body was still attached at its wheel base. I gingerly lifted the torn "skin" and bent down to look inside. The sleeve covering the locator on Robot's right side was still in place, but Fisher had accidentally severed the battery connection to the locator wire when he pulled out the circuit boards. The locator's little backup battery couldn't last much longer.

I reached into Robot's body and picked out the wire connecting the locator to the big battery. Fisher had left all his tools scattered around. It was easy to find the right one to splice the wire again.

It was all I could do for Robot. I longed to make it whole, but I knew it was more important to find Dad's laptop. My legs felt weak and trembly, so I steadied myself by holding the edge of the bench. It took all my strength to take my eyes off Robot and look around the crowded lab for the white laptop. Somehow, it never seemed as important as Robot, though I knew the laptop held the program that controlled Robot's every move.

The swish of an opening door startled me. I spun around to see a tall bony man coming through the door at the back of the lab. His curly blond hair framed a face that looked as if it had been colored with white chalk, and his eyes were as blue and cold as a winter sky. He could have been handsome, but he wasn't. He looked horrible.

I started to run, but he was too quick. Before I could get out of the lab, he grabbed me by the shoulders.

"Who's this?" His expression was blank, inscrutable. His even voice, pitched just above a whisper, sounded scarier than shouting. But I was too angry to be scared right then. I wanted to ask him the same question.

"You stole my robot!" I yelled, kicking out at him and trying to pull his hands away.

He held me tighter and cursed. "So you're Chow's kid. Came here all by yourself, did you? Who were you calling on the phone? There's no one home at your house."

I tried kicking him, but I couldn't get loose. What was he saying about the phone?

He put a leg around my feet and turned me to hold my back against his body as he pushed me out the door into the hallway. "But here you are. Now what am I going to do with you?"

Thumping and cursing sounded from the hall. Two figures wrestled their way toward us. Jude was trying to hold on to Tim. It was the first time I'd seen him up close without the blue knit cap. He had a bad case of acne, and his odor of sweat and unwashed hair was the same one I smelled in our house. He was having a hard time holding Tim, who is bigger and stronger than me.

"Chow's kid, too!" Jude cursed. I'm leaving out the swears, but let me tell you, these guys didn't have a big vocabulary.

"Who's that?" the blond man asked, looking at Tim. He couldn't talk very clearly while he was struggling with me. Points for me, but small ones.

"Chow's neighbor. Tim O'Mara." Jude panted. "Told you about him. Grilled Chow's kid for us. Gave us the cat and dog picture. Useful little twerp." He was having so much trouble holding Tim that he couldn't talk too well either. "Caught him in the office. What are we going to do with them? We have to get out of here!" Jude cursed some more.

"We could take them with us. Who knows what Chow told them about the prototype? They could be useful."

"Fisher!" Jude yelled now. His voice echoed up and down the hallway. "Have you lost your mind? I'm not heading to the slammer for you."

So Christian Fisher had not pretended to be Jude! Jude was really Jude, someone Fisher hired to spy on Dad.

Though we were bobbing and swaying, trying to get loose, Tim and I stared at each other for a second. Tears filled his eyes, his face flushed redder than it did at his house. He looked embarrassed and guilty, all at once.

"You're in this, whether you like it or not," Fisher spoke over my head. He was breathing hard, but his voice was still calm. "And if we have the kids, we can persuade Chow to spill." He twisted my arm viciously. I gasped with pain. "You'll get your share," he said, still looking at Jude.

"You're insane. You wanted Chow's robot. I got it for you. I'm not going to take the rap for kidnapping."

Kidnapping? My stomach twisted. My feet went icy cold. What would they do to us?

Try as I might, I couldn't break free. But I made it harder for Fisher to talk. He spit out, "I saw the phone light up. One of them made a call."

Jude answered, "I'm getting out of here fast. If you don't come with me, I'll let Tim loose. These kids weren't part of the deal."

Fisher pulled both my arms behind my back. It hurt so much I screamed. "Okay, okay, let's just leave them in the basement." He sneered at Jude. "Next time I'll know I should work alone."

I'm not repeating the names Jude and Fisher called me and Tim. They were grown men, way too strong for us. We couldn't get away, but because there were two of us, they couldn't let one go to tie the other up, so we kept struggling. Believe me, they weren't gentle as they took us through the front office, where Jude's pizza sat on the desk, getting cold, and then down the hall to the elevator.

The elevator took us down fast and the doors opened to an echoing cement room, a basement lobby with double metal doors on either side, closed tight. Fisher and Jude hustled us up to the doors on the left, marked Ultronics

Storage. I made a break while Fisher used one hand to rummage in his pocket for a key to unlock it, but then he tripped me so that I fell and skinned my knee and elbow on the hard cement floor. They grabbed me and threw me into a storage room, right behind Tim.

"A custodian will find you before you starve." Fisher smiled at me, his blue eyes bright and cold as ice. "Tell your dad I said hello."

The metal door clanged shut. Its echoes resounded through total darkness.

19

In the Dark

I sat up, hugging my knees. It didn't matter whether my eyes were open or closed. I couldn't see a thing. I heard Tim moving nearby, taking deep, jagged breaths. Myself, I was shaking with rage.

There were no words to describe how I felt about Christian Fisher, for what he did to Dad, for what he did to me, and most of all, for what he did to Robot. And I was angry at Tim for helping him. No matter what I said to Tim, or what I told myself, I knew that Robot was more than a machine. It was my friend, and I had loved it, for all its bossiness. I rubbed my wrists. They were still sore from Fisher's hard grip, and Jude's disgusting smell clung to my clothes.

"Tim!" I shouted into the dark. "You told! You showed Jude that picture, so he knew about Dad's vision work."

At first Tim's voice sounded small and choked, like he was struggling not to cry. "I wish I hadn't." Then it got louder and angrier. "But you made me so mad! You with your rich dad and your famous mom. You with your perfect life. You can buy anything you want. I have to work to get money to pay Ma back for a secondhand computer. You have a fancy robot that's all yours. You wouldn't even let me touch him!" I could hear him panting, trying to catch his breath.

"Jude said he worked for your dad's company, once." Tim's voice sounded clearer now. "Told me they treated him rotten, just like you were treating me. Jude liked robots, too. He told me he worked for another guy who built robots, and maybe that guy would give me one, if I helped him out." Tim let out one bitter hoot of laughter. "I guess he meant Fisher."

As my eyes got used to the dark, I could just see Tim's shape, sitting not too far away. We were locked in this room together, and I couldn't run away from him. Couldn't just ignore him.

"My life isn't perfect, no matter what you think!" I pushed my words, trying not to cry. "Dad made Robot as my baby-sitter, because he and Mom are too busy with their work to take care of me. That's what you could have told Jude about Robot! Dad wanted to see how much a robot could learn from being with me. All he cares about is his experiment. Not me!"

"At least you have a dad. And you're always so mean, you and your stuck-up friends!"

"You're the one who's mean!" I couldn't help it, I started to cry. "I may not even have a dad after this." I spoke through great gasping sobs. "Dad will be furious when he finds out I've lost his robot. He may never come back home. He likes being at work better, anyway. And he'll hate me forever now that Fisher has the white laptop, the one with Dad's secret program."

The last words came out in a wail. I put my head down on my knees. I couldn't talk anymore. All I could do was cry, while my thoughts raced like dark rain clouds.

Zumu might not have gotten to our house through all that snow, and Pablo could still be locked in the basement, just as I was now. I tried so hard to fix things, but I'd only made them worse. Much worse. All Dad's worrying, all the locks he'd built, couldn't keep us safe.

Tim edged over on his bottom to sit close to me. He patted me awkwardly on the back. "Hey, Celia, don't cry." He didn't whisper, so his voice sounded like a shout. "I'm really sorry for telling Jude so much. I was so stupid to believe he'd really give me a robot. I just liked talking about robots with someone. I promise, I never thought Jude would try to steal him. That's why I wanted to come with you. To make up for it."

I lifted my head and wiped my runny nose on my sleeve. Tim dug down into his pocket, and suddenly a dim light shone beside me. I could see Tim's face lit up by a tiny flashlight, the kind you put on key rings. His eyes looked all red and puffy.

He stuck the light close to the sun-and-moon watch on my wrist. "What time is it?"

I held up my watch so we could both see it. He was still breathing hard. "Four-fifteen," I said.

"Police should be here any minute. We can't keep

sitting like this. They'll never find us. I'm going to look for a light switch."

I watched, dazed, as he stood up, and shone the little light toward the door Fisher had slammed shut.

"Police?" I said weakly to his back.

Cursing must be infectious, because Tim did it too, once he found the light switch next to the door. "Doesn't work. They must have cut off the juice. I saw the fuse box outside."

I tried standing up, and found I could, though I was very unsteady. I reached out to support myself on the tall cardboard carton I'd been sitting against. I shivered with cold. All my muscles ached. I hugged my jacket around me.

Tim turned the doorknob and rattled the door. It held firm. "Think there's a phone down here?" he asked.

"What did you say about the police?" I asked again. I felt completely stupid, as if my thoughts were buried under layers of snow. I moved toward the door, slowly, trying not to stumble, then stopped as Tim started to feel his way around the basement.

The feeble light of Tim's flashlight played over metal shelves jammed with stuff I could barely see: cartons, wire, rolls of plastic sheeting, monitors and keyboards all jumbled together.

"Called the firehouse in West Haven while I watched for Jude." Tim sounded like he was out of breath. His foot clanged against the metal shelving, making an eerie ringing sound. "Told them where we were. Ted St. Pierre, my dad's best friend, said he'd contact the Boston police."

"So that's what Fisher meant. He must have seen a light on his office phone."

Tim wasn't listening. He held up the flashlight, playing its thin beam over the crowded, jumbled shelves, looking for a phone. I could see the side of his face, his cheek, and a bit of his hair in a small pool of light. I felt a tiny glimmer of hope.

"Tim, bring that light over here," I said. "I'll try to pick this lock."

"You . . . what?" Tim turned back. He probably couldn't see me.

"I have tools. Dad gave them to me," I called across the darkness. As he worked his way back, I added, "It's my hobby."

When Tim got close enough to see my lock-picking tools, he didn't ask any more questions. He just shone his tiny flashlight on the doorknob. I could see a keyhole in the middle of the doorknob. I took Tim's light and shone it through. It was locked from the inside.

I didn't waste time wondering why this door had an inside lock. Later I remembered the footprints in the snow on the night of Mom's concert and figured that Fisher was as big on security as Dad. He had the doors rigged so that he could come in his storage room through the outside loading dock, then unlock this door to get into the building's basement.

"There might be a key around here somewhere," I said. "If we find it, it would be easier than picking the lock."

Tim played his light on the dusty floor, littered with bits of wire and metal, and the shelves around the door. No key.

"If the police come and don't find us upstairs, they'll probably go away again," Tim said. "Then who knows how long we'll be here."

And Fisher will have a longer getaway time, I thought. Aloud, I said, "Okay, let's see what I can do."

I breathed deeply several times, the way Zumu did when she practiced tai chi. Be careful, move slowly, I told myself. If I dropped one of my tools, we'd have a hard time finding it in the dark with all the junk on the floor. Tim's flashlight gave off so little light that I could hardly see what I was doing.

It was an old-fashioned pin tumbler, no more than five pins. I slipped one finger in the envelope and pulled the picks out far enough to rub them with my thumb. A funny phrase popped into my head. *Never hurry, never worry.* As I slowly raised the pins to the shear line one by one, part of my brain was wondering where I'd heard that.

Oh, yes, *Charlotte's Web.* Remembering Mom reading to me broke my concentration for a moment. I knew she loved me, but I wasn't so sure she loved Dad. The pins inside the lock dropped. I tried again, but my hand was shaking so hard I couldn't get them back into a shear line.

"Good going, Celia," Tim said. I'm not sure he understood what I was doing, but he seemed to know I needed encouragement.

I pulled back, shook out my hand, breathed deeply, and tried again. This time I managed to raise all the pins. I felt inside my leather envelope for the right-sized torsion wrench to stick in. It slipped out of my cold fingers as I raised it to the lock, dropped, and made a small slapping noise as it hit the floor. The pins all fell back down.

I felt a stab of fear. We couldn't hear any sound from the floor above. The policemen could have come and gone already. Would we die of cold in this dark room?

"Hold still," Tim said. "I'll find it." I stood there rubbing my hands together to warm them up, while he knelt, playing his wobbly light over the floor.

It seemed like hours passed. Tim picked something up and held it to the light. A bit of wire. He cursed again and dropped it, and kept patting the floor. He pinched something long and dark and metal between his thumb and finger. As I looked at it, his flashlight flickered. The tiny battery was dying.

"A nail," I told him. "It looks like the torsion wrench, but it's not." Tim threw it down. He was working slowly and methodically, outward from the doorway. His fingers closed on something else. My torsion wrench!

"Here." He put the wrench—really a tiny bent metal straw—into my hand. Thinking how horrified Dad would be, I stuck that germy wrench between my teeth while I started on the lock for the fourth time. It took three more tries to get all the pins raised.

I stuck in the wrench. It moved freely inside the tumbler.

Holding my breath, I tried the knob. It turned.

The door to our basement prison swung open. Bright light seemed to bang against my eyeballs. Tim stumbled out beside me. I stuffed my tools back into their leather envelope and slipped them into my inside jacket pocket. We were free!

Tim pointed to a door with the familiar Exit sign. "Stairs are faster," he panted. And safer, I thought as I ran after him. I hated the idea of getting inside a little box I couldn't control. I didn't want to be locked in again.

When we got to the first floor, Tim rushed out of the stairwell and across the lobby to fling open the front door. "They made it!" I heard him shout.

The flashing red light on top of a police car parked at the curb looked like a brilliant spotlight in the winter night. A policeman swung out of the driver's seat as soon as he saw Tim. I followed Tim into the cold air, shivering and fumbling in my pockets to find my mittens and hat as my feet slipped over snow. The driveway beside the building was empty. Uneven mounds of snow lined each side. The blue van had disappeared.

"You must be the kids from West Haven," the policeman said. "Where were you? The other guys didn't find you upstairs."

"They locked us in the basement." Tim sounded as angry as I felt. He pointed to the driveway. "They got away!"

But the officer was already talking on his car radio. "The kids are down here," I heard him say. "They're safe."

I grabbed his arm. "Please," I said. "I need to call

home. My parents are away, but I think my grandmother's there. She'll be worried."

He had a dark round face and kind brown eyes that seemed to really see me for the first time. "Let's get you both inside where it's warmer." Once we were back in the lobby, he handed me a cell phone. "Only some parts of West Haven have power," he said. "Don't know about your block."

I was so trembly and tired and my fingers were so stiff that I had trouble pressing the tiny buttons. I seemed to wait forever before our home phone started ringing. When I heard Zumu's voice, I almost sobbed with relief. She sounded guarded, the way she does when she doesn't know who's calling.

"Zumu," I said, "I found Robot."

Before I could say anything more, she exploded into Chinese. And then, "Celia, where are you?"

"I'm near Omei, in Cambridge. The police are with us."

"Already called police. Came here. Robot not important. Only you! You okay? When you come home?" Zumu fired words like gunshots. When she got that upset, her English sounded like Chinese. She spoke so loudly that Tim and the officer could hear her.

"Tell your grandma you'll be home soon," the officer said. "We have another squad car waiting at the station."

"I'm okay," I told her. "The police will bring me home."

She burst into Chinese again. Some proverb, I think. Her voice sounded calmer. "Your dad and mom come back soon."

Then Tim called his mom, but she wasn't home. The officer said that someone at the station would keep trying.

After that, the policemen took charge. One of them came out of the elevator while Tim was calling. He smiled as he introduced himself: "Sergeant Jefferson. We'd like to ask you a few questions upstairs." He looked at us intently. "If you're both okay."

"We're okay," I said, looking at Tim. He nodded, wiping his nose with the back of his hand.

Sergeant Jefferson took us up on the elevator, but I didn't feel so trapped there while he was with us. The Ultronics front office blazed with light. We went into Fisher's lab, where another policeman stood, writing things down. Even with those two kind policemen, I felt scared and angry all over again, remembering how that horrible man had grabbed me.

Sergeant Jefferson asked each of us to tell everything that happened in the Ultronics office. While Tim was talking, I looked around the lab, hoping to see pieces of Robot left behind. The lab was an even bigger mess. I showed the police where Robot had been. We described the van and gave them the plate number. I told them about the locator, and they said they were already trying to trace it.

"They've got a good head start on us, but we should be able to get them and recover your dad's invention," Sergeant Jefferson said.

Streetlights shone on the tiny, snow-covered front yards of white clapboard houses as the car wound through narrow streets on its way to the police station. After a woman at the desk took our addresses, we got into a squad car with the officer who had first greeted us. By then we knew his name: Sergeant Le Guin. He drove along Memorial Drive, between Harvard dormitories and the Charles River. The lights of Boston, on the other side of the river, shimmered on the dark water.

Then we were passing big houses. The streets and sidewalks had been plowed, and mountains of snow along the edges made them narrower. I imagined happy families inside those lighted windows. I envied them. I felt numb—numb with cold, numb with defeat. If I'd been able to rescue Robot, or even bring back Dad's laptop, I might have a happy family, just for that night. But Dad would not be happy tonight. He'd be furious.

I heard static and radio voices up front. Sergeant Le Guin turned his head to say, "Tim, they reached your mom. She's waiting at home."

I think I might have dozed off for a few minutes, because it seemed like no time had passed before we were driving along Woodland Road. The car parked in Tim's driveway. He sat there in the backseat, looking at me. "They'll get Robot back, you'll see," he said. "And when they do, I want to know about it."

I felt like I was encased in glass. His mother, in her white uniform, stood in the open doorway of their little house. "Bye, Tim," I said. I added, because I knew I should, "Thanks for everything."

I watched Sergeant Le Guin escort him to the door and straight into his mother's arms. We backed out of

Tim's driveway and drove up Heartwright Lane. Light streamed from every window of our house, shining across mounds of snow.

Heartwright Lane had been plowed, and so had our driveway. I was tired, muddled, and drifting off when I saw something that scared me awake.

Dad's Volvo sat in the driveway. I would have to face him right away.

20

Using Chopsticks

Dad stood in the open doorway, a black silhouette against the light glowing behind him. I couldn't see his face as I came up the walk, with Sergeant Le Guin holding my arm to keep me from stumbling. Dad reached out to help me through the door. In the light from the doorway I could see his face. His eyes glittered dangerously. He wasn't smiling, he wasn't frowning. I couldn't tell if he was really mad or just annoyed. He held me steady as I crossed the threshold, then propelled me to the bench in the vestibule. "Take off boots," he said, sounding angry.

Suddenly a crowd filled the vestibule. Zumu burst out of the kitchen to help me pull off my boots and take off my coat. She spoke in her quick Shanghai dialect that sounded like scolding. Dad, not me. She'd scold me in English. Dad wasn't listening to her, because Mr. Weissman came out of the living room at the same time Dad asked Sergeant Le Guin to come in. Then Dad closed the front door and stood with his back against it. His hair was messy and his shirt had come untucked from his pants. He looked trembly and pale. I could see how upset he was about losing Robot.

"... never would have found them, but your girl picked a lock," Sergeant Le Guin was saying.

Zumu put slippers on my feet and pulled me up from the bench. I turned around and stood in the circle of her arms, my back pressed against her. Big, calm Sergeant Le Guin seemed like a rock as he listened to the crackling voices on his radio while Dad and Mr. Weissman raged.

"I thought Parmenter was a slime when I fired him, but I never thought he was this nasty. Teaming up with Fisher!" That was Mr. Weissman.

Dad's eyes opened wide. "Jude worked for Moria?"

"For about six months, in shipping. Claimed he wanted to build robots. Left just after you came. Kept appropriating the inventory."

"We should charge them both with assault and put them away." Dad tucked his shirt in, sounding cold and angry.

Sergeant Le Guin stuck his radio into the pocket on his shoulder. "We've got a bead on the locator. Rhode Island Highway Patrol is closing in on the van."

He looked straight at me. "They never pulled a gun on you, right?"

Zumu tightened her arms around me. Dad made a strange, strangled gasping sound, but stood stiff and still. I shook my head. "I don't think they had one," I whispered.

Sergeant Le Guin's lips curved in the ghost of a smile. "Dangerous but probably not armed. We should have them, and the stolen property, in custody soon. I think we have all your numbers. We'll let you know when there's something to report." As he went out the door, he said to Dad, "That's one smart girl you have."

Dad looked down at me. I could see tears sliding down his cheeks now. My throat went tight. I'd never seen Dad cry. "Celia, you shouldn't have risked . . ." He couldn't finish the sentence.

"Well, Alex, I'd better hit the road." Mr. Weissman looked really embarrassed.

"No, no." Zumu exploded like she was speaking Chinese. I could feel her making an effort to slow down and sound more American. "Chinese food be here any minute. Order from Four Seas. You don't go home to empty house. Stay. Eat with us."

Dad wiped his cheeks with the back of his hand. "Yes, Caleb. Stay for dinner. There's still a lot to sort out."

"I get ready." Zumu retreated to the kitchen, leaving me in the entry hall with Dad and Mr. Weissman.

"He cut Robot to pieces. And he took your laptop." My voice sounded loud and shaky. I did not want to start crying. "I couldn't do anything, just reconnect the locator's battery. He's found out all your secrets!"

Dad reached out and patted me awkwardly on the shoulder. "Celia, you know we can build another robot." His voice started to shake. "But not you. Can't build another you."

I leaned against Dad, limp with relief, and hugged him tight. He wasn't mad at me for losing Robot.

I heard Mr. Weissman say, "Besides, I don't think Fisher could ever replicate the interactivity." He meant what Robot learned from me.

A jungle howl, muffled but urgent, sounded through the kitchen.

"Pablo!" I yelled. I slipped away from Dad and ran past Zumu to open the basement door. Pablo rushed out. He didn't look at me, and he didn't purr when I tried to stroke him. In all the confusion, Zumu had forgotten him. He was furious about being left in the basement. I guess he'd been so scared down there, he didn't meow until he heard my voice. I picked him up, planning to carry him into the living room, when headlights beamed through the kitchen windows. A car motor rumbled outside.

Zumu stopped laying out plates on the dining room table and rushed to the front door, saying, *"Fan lai le,"* or "Food is here." She had to take short steps because she still wore her tight Chinese teaching dress.

I looked out the kitchen window and put Pablo down. A car was parked in our driveway, all right—a shiny black car, with lots of chrome. But the person getting out of it was not a man swinging plastic bags filled with boxes of rice and stir-fry.

It was Mom. I ran to the vestibule and met her just as she was coming through the front door.

She threw her arms around me, wrapping me in her soft winter coat, her loose blond hair swirling around my cheeks. She smelled of cold snow and the sour inside of the car. I could feel her shaking and I couldn't hold back my tears any longer. They came out in a rush, and with them all my guilt and anger and fear. At that moment, I realized how much danger I had been in.

Mom kept whispering, "Celia, Celia."

No sooner had Dad closed the front door than he heard a loud knock and had to open it again. A man wearing a cap and a faded dark jacket stood outside, holding Mom's cello case. "Lady left this in the car," he said, holding out the cello. "Thought she'd come back."

Dad rummaged in his pocket and pulled out a bill. "Thanks for your trouble," he said. "She's a little shaken up."

As he said this, a horn tooted from the end of the driveway.

"Fan lai le!" Zumu called out once again. This time she was right. She went out to yell in Chinese at the driver of a little red car. The Four Seas delivery man backed up to let the black car out, then pulled up beside our door. Two Chinese men lugged in large plastic sacks stuffed with white boxes. Zumu issued orders. She was telling them where to put things, and to be careful. They had to make two trips to bring in all the food.

While the men rushed back and forth, Dad and Mom stood in one corner of the vestibule, hugging each other. They are about the same height, and their two heads, black-haired and blond, rested side by side. Dad might have whispered in her ear, but I couldn't hear him. Then he helped Mom take off her coat and hung it up for her as she rummaged in her pocket for tissues to dry our tears.

She stared vacantly at the kitchen where Zumu was bustling about. Mom looked dazed, as if she'd never seen our house before. She reached for my hand.

Now our house was warm and light and filled with people and good smells. Dad looked more like himself. "There's enough food for twenty people!" he said to Zumu.

I was still sniffling, but I felt better too. Thawing out. "Can we invite Tim and his mom?" I asked.

"Good idea," Mom said, like someone who's just woken up. "I'll call Maureen right now."

So there I was, sitting at our dining room table, showing Tim how to use chopsticks. "You hold two in one hand to get the food to your mouth. Keep the bottom one steady," I told him, scissoring my chopsticks to show him. "It's easier if you put the meat over your rice and eat them together." I scooped some shrimp from one of the white boxes and dumped it over my rice to demonstrate.

While Tim and his mom and I had been laying out rice bowls and chopsticks and finding enough glasses and teacups, Zumu had been making tea, and Dad and Mr. Weissman had brought up beer from the basement. Dad raised his glass. "To Celia and Tim," he said. "You found the crooks, and got home safely."

All the grown-ups raised their glasses, smiling at us and echoing Dad's toast. Mom was crying again. Dad didn't drink, which meant he had more to say. He held his glass and looked straight into my eyes. "You were very brave, and very foolish. Don't *ever* do anything like that again!"

"If Jude and Fisher hadn't killed you, you could have died in that basement." Mr. Weissman sounded very stern.

At that moment, I felt all mixed up. I wanted Dad to admire me for saving Robot, not scold me.

"They thought the custodian would find us in the morning," Tim said.

"How did the police know you were there?" Mr. Weissman asked.

"While Celia checked out the lab, I stayed in the front office and figured out how to use the phone." Tim looked at his mom. "I called the fire department. Ted answered."

"Ted St. Pierre, a friend of his dad's," Mrs. O'Mara explained to the other grown-ups.

"Why did you call the West Haven Fire Department instead of the Boston police?" Mom asked.

"Celia called the police earlier and they didn't believe her, and I had to get help fast. I thought Jude might be back any minute."

"Boston's finest." Mr. Weissman smiled ironically.

"They get a lot of prank calls." Mrs. O'Mara looked at Mr. Weissman severely. "Especially on a snow day with kids home from school."

"We thought Jude was the only person there," I said. "But M-Mr.—" I stuttered. I didn't want to start crying again, but just trying to say Fisher's name set me off. I kept thinking of Robot, all dismembered. "He was in his office." I gulped. "He grabbed me before I could find the laptop."

"Fisher wanted to beat us out for the recycling contract—" Mr. Weissman said.

"So he sent Jude to spy on your house," Tim interrupted. Everyone at the table looked at him, startled.

"Spy?" Mr. Weissman asked.

"Yeah. Jude and Mark Ludlow were high school buddies. Jude's been hanging around all winter. He kept asking me if I'd seen Celia's robot, and what it could do. I felt so stupid because I hardly knew anything. He told me to ask Celia questions. He said his boss might give me a robot if I helped him out."

"So Fisher wanted more than the contract. He tried to steal systems he couldn't create on his own." Mr. Weissman put down his chopsticks and looked straight at Dad. "Like a vision system that can tell a cat from a dog."

"How did he know about that?" Dad asked.

Tim paused, swallowing. I could see him getting up his courage. "I showed him the picture from the paper."

"Picture?" Dad and Mr. Weissman spoke together.

Tim stared down at his plate. He didn't look as if he could say anymore. It was my turn to confess. "*The Villager* published a picture of Robot grabbing the cat away from the dog. I said in a small voice. "I was in it, too."

"What?" Dad and Mr. Weissman stared at me.

I meant to tell the truth straight out, but then I started to cry again, and everything came out all muddled. Tim found his voice again and told his part of the story. When the grown-ups finally realized what had happened, they all spoke at once.

"Not your fault!" Zumu said to me, looking angrily at Dad.

"They would have found out sooner or later," Mr. Weissman said.

"Celia, there's no way you're responsible for what those two creeps did," Dad told me. I felt a huge weight lift off my shoulders. I'd been so afraid Dad would blame me forever when he found out about the picture.

"We can't blame Tim, either," said Mr. Weissman. "He didn't really know what they were up to."

Mom reached over to rub my shoulders, but looked at Dad. "I helped them without meaning to. Celia found Jude lurking around our house. He said he was after Rocky. I believed him and didn't tell you, Alex, because I was afraid you'd make a big scene."

"If you had known then what you know now, would you have done what you did?" Dad grinned. It was an old joke. He was repeating an English phrase that's very hard to say in Chinese, because Chinese verbs have no tenses. In his own way, Dad was trying to make Mom feel better.

Mr. Weissman dumped rice from a white carton into his bowl, and mixed it with some chicken and cashews. "Instead of going back to his lab, Fisher will probably go directly to jail. Celia and Tim got him out of our hair permanently. The recycling contract's ours for the asking, thanks to them."

"Right," Dad said. He locked eyes with Tim, then with me, and spoke slowly and seriously. "But if something had happened to either one of you . . ." His voice gave out.

Mr. Weissman finished his sentence. "Do you think we would care one bit about that recycling contract, no matter how many millions it's worth?"

He eyed Dad, who was nodding, and went on. "You two kids are more valuable than any contract could ever be. Celia, you've made such progress in interactivity—"

Dad interrupted, punching his chopsticks in the air. "But you more important than experiment." He paused for a moment, looked at Mrs. O'Mara, and added, "Tim too."

By now, the boxes of food were half empty. Dad picked out a tidbit or two with his chopsticks. I watched him, thinking that I felt more tired than I had ever been in my life. My skinned knee and elbow throbbed. My muscles started aching all over. I leaned against Mom, and she put her arm around me.

"I think it's time we got these kids to bed," she said to Mrs. O'Mara.

Mr. Weissman said he'd drop off Tim and Mrs. O'Mara on his way home. Zumu and Dad started cleaning up. I could hear Zumu speaking to Dad in Chinese. Her voice sounded loud and strong, like she was lecturing him.

They kept talking while Mom did something she hadn't done since I was in kindergarten. She helped me undress, ran a bathtub of hot water, and while I was soaking, turned down my bed. She toweled me dry, dropped a clean nightgown over my head, and brushed my hair.

"Mom, you were supposed to be playing tonight."

"Herb Goldman had to propose to his sweetie without me." She smiled. "When I called home and Zumu told me you were missing, they demanded that I stay." Her voice got high as she imitated Lila. "Your girl's just gone off with a friend. We have a job to do." Her voice dropped. "I called my driver and they did the job without me. Calyx will have to find another cellist."

She plumped up my pillow and held back the comforter while I snuggled into bed. She sat beside me. "I did a lot of thinking on the drive home," she said. "I'm going to audition for the Walden Chamber Orchestra. If I don't get a chair, I'll do some solo work and teaching. I want to stay closer to home for the next few years." She tucked the covers around me and smoothed my hair back. "Want me to read to you?"

"That's all right," I mumbled, because I was so sleepy I could hardly talk. I knew I'd fall asleep while she was reading.

She turned out the light. "Do you miss Robot?"

"Sure." In its bossy way, Robot had helped me a lot, but that wasn't why I missed it. I was beginning to understand that it had learned from me as well. Dad had designed it to interact with me, to really be my friend. I knew it would never be quite the same friend again. I remembered how Robot's blue light had kept me company in the dark room. Then I remembered something else. "Happy Valentine's Day," I whispered.

"Thanks for the valentine." Mom hugged me and kissed my cheek. "I found it on my dresser."

She sat beside me in the dark for a while, humming an old lullaby about a baby sailing away on a silver moon. I was almost asleep when she left.

Then Pablo sneaked into my room and burrowed under the covers, purring richly. I guess he'd forgiven me. He turned around and kneaded until he had found the right spot.

Because of Pablo, I heard Mom join the conversation between Zumu and Dad. I couldn't understand what she was saying, but she didn't sound upset. The conversation just continued in a mixture of English and Chinese. Zumu kept saying something over and over. Dad translated for Mom. "'Pearl on the palm.' A Chinese name for an only daughter."

That was the last thing I heard before I fell asleep.

21

My Big Idea

Mr. Weissman brought the company lawyer over the next afternoon. After she had asked me a million questions and recorded my answers on tape, they went over to Tim's house to ask him a million more. Mr. Weissman returned to our house by himself, because Zumu had invited him to help us eat leftover Chinese food. He told me that Tim's deposition was recorded. I asked if I could have a copy of the tape.

"What do you want it for?" Mr. Weissman asked.

"I have an idea," I answered. "I don't want to tell you about it now, but I need that tape to make it work." My idea had come to me the minute I woke up. It was a big, big idea, but I wasn't ready to talk about it yet.

Mr. Weissman nodded. I think he guessed right then what was on my mind.

It was dark by the time Dad's Volvo rolled up Heartwright Lane. He burst through the door, clutching his white laptop to his chest, and announced with a huge grin, "We've got it! And Fisher's in the slammer."

Everyone asked questions at once. Dad told us that the Rhode Island Highway Patrol had followed the locator and pulled the blue van over on I-95. Later, I had to identify Fisher and Jude over closed circuit TV. I got sick to my stomach just looking at their faces. They were charged with theft and assault. Tim thought they deserved a life sentence, but I wasn't so sure.

They didn't stay in prison long, because Mr. Weissman made Mr. Fisher pay damages and agree to something called an injunction, which meant he had to stay away from Moria Systems. After he was released from prison, he headed for the West Coast, and we never heard of him again. Jude also had to stay away. He went down to Florida to work for another computer company. "Never even asked for references," Mr. Weissman joked.

While we ate dinner, Mr. Weissman told us what he thought of Tim, which gave me a chance to prepare Dad for my idea. "That boy's a lot like me when I was a kid," Mr. Weissman told us. "Bright, but no outlet, no opportunities."

"Dad, will you let Tim help put Robot back together again?" My idea was bigger than that, but I had to start somewhere.

Mr. Weissman beamed at me. "Didn't I tell you Celia was one smart girl? That's an excellent suggestion."

Dad looked very dubious. "He doesn't know anything."

"Alex!" Mom said. "He saved Celia's life! Surely you can teach him."

"Maybe."

"Dad, you've got to promise."

"Alex, I second that," Mr. Weissman said.

"Okay, okay." Dad held up his open hands in mock defeat.

After Zumu left on Sunday, we were back to normal, sort of. Normal like before Robot came. Pablo kept padding around the house. He couldn't settle down. I actually think he was looking for Robot. The house seemed lonely without that bossy plastic canister, but its reminders were hardwired in my brain. I would never again forget to hang up my clothes and make my bed.

And Mom was home all the time. She still practiced, but she didn't lock herself in the guest room so much any more. She left the door open, or played duets with me. Though I still hadn't found the right moment to tell Dad my idea, Mom faced him head on with an idea of her own.

At dinner Monday night, she said, "Alex, we still need someone to stay with Celia after school and tidy up. I've quit Calyx, but I haven't given up the cello."

Dad said that once we'd repaired Robot, it could do the job, but she stood firm. "Celia doesn't need a baby-sitter, but we need a human being," she said, more than once. "Mrs. Le Beck has been in town for years. She's known most of her workers since they were born. The McMahons use her service, and I'm sure we can trust anyone she sends."

Mom kept up until Dad agreed, and now the house looks a whole lot tidier.

Mom drove me to and from school all that week, so I didn't see much of Tim. He couldn't go up the hill to work for Mark, because Dad called Mrs. Prentice in Florida to tell her about Mark and Jude. She fired Mark and hired a new caretaker, Mrs. Le Beck's son, who didn't need Tim's help.

On Wednesday, I found Tim alone near his locker. "Dad promised to let you help us repair Robot," I whispered. "We're going to start this Friday."

He looked at me, startled, when the late bell rang. "Wow! That's great," he blurted out over his shoulder as he trotted down the hall to his class.

When Dad picked me up that cold, blustery Friday, the backseat of his car was filled with big plastic trunks, the same ones he'd brought in when he first built Robot. Robot's pieces were inside those boxes.

"Can we start tonight?" I asked. "I'll call Tim as soon as we get home."

"If you finish your homework, we can get it laid out before bedtime," Dad said. He sounded a lot like Robot. "I don't think we need Tim tonight."

"Dad, you promised!" You have to keep after Dad. He really didn't want to let Tim into his workshop, but he did that night.

When Dad lifted the pieces that were once Robot out of the box, Tim looked like he was going to cry. I felt like bursting into tears, too, but I didn't want to make things worse. When Dad saw how carefully Tim followed his instructions as we laid out all the jumbled pieces of plastic, tubing, and circuit boards on the workbench, he began to change the way he treated Tim.

Then I knew I could tell Dad about my idea. Mom slept late on Saturday morning, so Dad and I had breakfast together.

"Dad, I have something really important to ask you." That got his attention. I looked straight into his eyes, gathered my courage, and spoke.

"When Robot is repaired, can we let Tim have it?"

Dad sat silent for a long minute. I couldn't tell what he was thinking. Finally he said, "You want to give your robot to Tim? Why?"

My reasons came out in a rush, before Dad could interrupt. "Tim wants a robot of his own in the worst way. Jude promised him one as a kind of bribe. And he needs Robot more than I do now. He needs Robot to make him feel important. He must be so bored home alone all the time. That's partly why he went up to help Mark Ludlow. Now that you've been working with him, you've seen how smart he is. If he had Robot to help him, he might do his homework and get better grades. And he needs to figure out it's a machine and not a person. I can go visit Robot at his house anytime. Besides, Robot is your first prototype, and you can always make a second prototype for me."

Dad stared at me for a long moment. He looked so strange that I was afraid he might start crying. He swallowed very hard. Then he said, "I'd have to reprogram the voice recognition."

He just said yes, I thought in amazement. "Mr. Weissman said he'd give you a tape of Tim's depo . . . depo . . ."

"Deposition. Of course," Dad said. "It's a start. And Tim can also interact with Robot verbally. But I don't think we should tell him right away. Let's see how well the repairs go, and surprise him."

Dad kept his promise to assemble Robot on evenings and weekends, when we could help. Sometimes Dad got impatient, but after a while he seemed to like having us around. Eventually, he showed me how to unlock his workshop door so that Tim and I could work on Robot after school, before Dad came home. I promised him I would always finish my homework before bedtime, and I always did.

The only thing Dad did by himself was reprogram the voice recognition software, using the tape of Tim's deposition. We had to give Robot a completely new body. The old one was just too mangled. We made it out of shining silvery metal, decorated with black rectangles. Robot's new body was longer and slimmer, its switches sleeker, its arms more flexible. We decided it didn't need a video monitor and keyboard. Dad made its voice a little gentler too, but it still had the same shimmering brown globes for eyes. It's like a grown-up version of the old robot.

While Dad got the vision system going again, which took really complex programming on the laptop, Tim and I created simpler software. We programmed New Robot not to be so bossy, to give choices instead of commands. Even

Dad wasn't sure how much it would "remember" the things I had taught it. "We'll just have to watch it and see," he said.

That night we found out it could still sing "Deck the Halls." Dad said, *"Ding hao!"* with a thumbs-up sign, and we all gave each other high fives.

Then Dad looked at me and said, "It's time to activate the voice recognition system. Celia, are you ready?"

When he handed me the remote, my heart seemed to get all squeezed up. I knew I was going to miss my bossy old Robot.

New Robot turned slightly, to face Tim. "Hello, Timothy O'Mara. I am your robot now."

Tim's eyes opened wide and his face got red. He looked at Dad, and then at me, and then back at Dad again, his mouth hanging open. He stammered, "Y-You're g-giving me . . ."

Dad and I both smiled and nodded. "Technically, it's a loaner," Dad said. "I'll keep its programs on my laptop, so it will have to come back and forth. Celia thinks you need it more than she does."

Then a big grin spread over Tim's face. He raised his arms over his head like a champion, shouting, "Wow, oh wow!" We high-fived all over again. My heart opened up, and I didn't feel quite so bad about losing Robot.

School is almost over now. Tim has had New Robot for three months, and he's taught it to do things I wouldn't think of, like pitching a ball for batting practice. That means he's taken it outside on the lawn between us and the McMahons. Dad grumbled, until he saw how well New Robot could pitch.

This summer, Tim and I are going to a two-week summer camp in robotics at MIT. Mr. Weissman will pay Tim's tuition, and he's given him a retainer fee for "interactive development." That means talking to New Robot. Not only that, he bought Tim a laptop computer. I just watched them set it up. Mr. Weissman told Tim, "Stay home and do your math homework." Then he put his hands on both our shoulders. "You two are the future." He looked at us very seriously. "Believe in yourselves. Take care of yourselves. The world has so many problems. Maybe you will help solve one or two of them."

As Mr. Weissman and I started to leave, Tim said, "Hey Mr. W., you ever play baseball?"

So that's how we all ended up playing stickball together, on this warm May evening. Mom is home from rehearsal with the Walden Chamber Orchestra, where she has a chair, and takes over second base. Mrs. O'Mara has been home long enough to change out of her nurse's uniform into slacks. Mom gets her to play third. "We moms have to stick together," she says. Dad decides to play first base. He never told me he had played first in Taiwan Little League, and again in Brookline.

"That leaves me the only fielder." Mr. Weissman pulls out his shirt and stands somewhere between shortstop and center field. Tim's the catcher and I'm at bat, wearing the Red Sox cap Tim gave me for my fourth birthday. Mom couldn't bear to give it away, so she kept it in her dresser drawer. When she saw that Tim and I were going to be friends, she gave it back to me, and I sometimes wear it, even though it's too small.

Maeve teases me about having a boyfriend, and Jennifer asks how I can stand to be around him. I explain that Tim is not my boyfriend, but he is my friend, because he helped me find Robot. I say that he acted like a bully because he didn't know how else to act, and besides, he was jealous of me for having a dad and a robot and all the other stuff I have, including computers. I tell them I jumped to the conclusion that he was a mean bully, but I was wrong. "He acts different when he's doing something he likes," I said.

Tim is the only one I know who's as interested in computers as I am, and who knows as much about them. I'm glad he has New Robot, though sometimes I miss the old one sitting next to my bed. I can still play imaginative games and talk about books with Maeve, and I still like to gossip and do my homework with Jennifer. And next year we'll be sixth graders together. Instead of two best friends, I have three, even though Tim isn't friends with my girlfriends. Next year he'll be in middle school, which is good, because at Abigail Adams everyone expects us to behave a certain way. When we work on robots, we can just be ourselves.

New Robot pitches me the ball, and I miss. "Strike one!" everybody shouts.

Dad yells, "Keep your eye on the ball!" He's happy

because he's hard at work on a second prototype of Robot. He's programming it to help Zumu teach me Chinese.

I try, but I miss again. If I don't get a hit, it will be Mr. Weissman's turn at bat and I'll have to go out into the field, which means all the batters will get home runs, because I'm such a terrible fielder.

Instead of throwing the ball back to New Robot, Tim runs over and hands it the ball. Then he runs back behind me and yells, "Throw!"

The ball comes to me. I connect, drop the broomstick, and start running. But I don't make it to first base, because Pablo streaks right across my path. Zumu, who had been cooking dinner in the kitchen, had opened the door to watch the game, and he got out. All the activity and shouting has made him wild. I jump to avoid him, trip, and roll over on the grass.

Dad runs toward me but I get up, laughing. I have grass stains on my T-shirt and pants, and my hat falls off. Mom has caught Pablo and she's holding him tight. He's switching his tail, and his ears are back. When Mom sees me laughing, she starts to laugh too. Mr. Weissman shouts, "Error, error!" and Dad yells, "Try again, Celia."

"Time out!" Mom cries, and carries Pablo back into the house. Zumu stays outside, smiling. I put my cap on New Robot's dome and go back to home plate.

Tim takes the ball back to his robot. It stands tall and serene amid all the confusion. Mom gets back to position. New Robot holds the ball, waiting for Tim's command. I look straight into its shimmering brown globes, focused on me.

"Throw," Tim orders.

Everyone's watching me. They're all rooting for me, whether I get a hit or not. I take a deep breath, and wait for what comes.

MARGARET CHANG has coauthored children's books set in China with her husband. A former children's librarian, she has taught undergraduate and graduate courses in children's literature. She lives in Williamstown, Massachusetts.